UNFINISHED BUSINESS

THE HARRY STARKE NOVELS
BOOK 24

BLAIR HOWARD

Blair Howard Books

For Jo
As Always

1

Friday July 12, 2001

10:43PM

"WHERE THE HELL have you been, you son of a bitch?" she yelled as he walked through the front door. "Out whoring again? Another slut was it? I ought to cut your frickin' dick off, you disgusting pervert. I hope you catch something nasty, and it rots and drops off," she ranted.

He slammed the door. "Shut your damn mouth, you crazy bitch," he retorted. "You'll wake the frickin' kids and the neighbors. Where I've been and who I've been with is no concern of yours."

"You're sick," she snarled. "You need help. You need to see someone."

"Get the hell out of my way," he snapped, pushing past her. "I need a drink."

She followed him into the living room.

He glanced back at her as he filled a shot glass with tequila, downed it, then another, and finally a third before taking a deep breath and turning to look at her, his lips clamped tight together, his eyes narrowed, then he said, "Let it go, will you?"

She stared up at him. "Who is it?" she asked. "What's the bitch's name?"

He glared at her but said nothing.

"This has got to stop!" she shouted. Her voice trembled. "I can't stand it anymore. You have to stop. It's disgusting. You… You're a… pervert."

"Me? ME?" he shouted. "I'm a pervert? What about you? When did we…? You frigid bitch! When did we last…? I don't even remember; it's been so long. I have needs. If you… I wouldn't have to… if you…" He shook his head. "If you'd provide what I need, I wouldn't have to go elsewhere for it. Would I?"

"You blame me?" she yelled. "Really? Really? You've got to be kidding! You think for one minute I'm going to let you stick that stinking thing in me? Hell no! Who the hell knows where it's been?" She paused for a moment, then lowered her voice, shook her head, then whispered, "You need help!"

He stuck out his jaw, glaring at her, then he calmed down a little and said, "I was here all night. Understand?"

She stared at him, her mouth open, her eyes wide.

"I said, do you UNDERSTAND?" he shouted.

She jumped, startled, then nodded her head. "What? Why?" Where have you been?" she asked again, and then she noticed the state he was in. She narrowed her eyes, frowning, and said, "Your clothes. They're filthy… Oh my God. What have you done?"

"What d'you mean, what have I done?" he snarled. "I've done nothing. I was here all night," he repeated. "Just remember that. Now let it go."

"Mom? Dad? What the hell's going on?"

They both turned to see their youngest son standing in the doorway.

"It's your father," his mother said. "He's been up to his tricks again. God only knows what he's done this time. Go on back to bed. I'll handle it, and don't tell your brother. I have enough on my plate without that."

He watched as his son turned slowly away and went back up the stairs.

"Keep your voice down," his wife said. "What they must think of you…" She shook her head in disgust, then turned and followed her son up the stairs.

"Bitch!" he said as he glanced at the clock on the mantlepiece. It was two minutes after eleven. He turned on the TV. The late-night news had just started. It was raining. The female reporter was standing under an umbrella, blue and red lights flashing in the background.

"… the body of a young woman…"

He turned the TV off, sat down heavily in the over-stuffed, over-sized recliner, laid his head back, closed his eyes, and shuddered.

2

Friday October 21, 2022

It was one of those balmy days in late October. The weather was exceptional: temperatures were in the mid-seventies. There was a light breeze blowing. The azure sky was dotted with fluffy white clouds, and I hadn't a care in the world. I was at lunch at the Acropolis with Amanda and Jade. It was a pleasant moment.

It was also a Friday, the end of a near perfect week. We'd closed out two difficult cases, taken on a new legal client—one of Chattanooga's most prominent law firms—and I was looking forward to taking it easy for a few days.

Halloween was just a few days away, and Jade was looking forward to trick or treating. Amanda had already found her an outfit: Princess Leia.

Anyway, we were just finishing our lunch and were discussing what we were going to do over the weekend. Jade insisted on babbling about her preschool and her friends—she'd gotten out early that day—and was demanding a sleepover. Me? I'd already arranged to play golf with my father, August Starke, Judge Henry

Strange and ADA Larry Spruce on the Sunday, but planned to just lounge around the house and pool and relax on the Saturday. Amanda had co-opted Maria to look after Jade on Saturday while she met with her best friend, Louise McArthur. She and Jade would meet us at the club for lunch.

I tell you all this because, as you might imagine, I was looking forward to an idyllic weekend with my family. Sadly, it was not to be.

We were on our second cup of coffee when my cell phone vibrated in my pocket. I took it out and looked at the screen. It was Jacque, my PA and business partner.

I looked at Amanda, took a deep breath, closed my eyes, and said, "It's Jacque!"

"Don't answer it, Daddy," Jade shouted, turning heads all around the restaurant.

I shook my head. "Better take it," I said. "She wouldn't call unless it was important."

She nodded, but didn't answer, though she did put her finger to her lips for Jade to keep quiet.

I tapped the screen and said, "Jacque. This had better be good. I'm having lunch with my family."

"Good? I'm not so sure about dat," she replied.

Jacque is my PA and business partner. She's special to me. Jamaican by birth and thirty-five years old, she doesn't look a day older than twenty. She's tall—five nine—has beautiful skin the color of coffee and cream, bushy black hair, and a captivating smile. She has a master's degree in business administration and a bachelor's in criminology. She's assertive, self-assured, and incredibly smart. She runs the agency like a well-oiled clock. She's also protective of me, our reputation, my privacy, and my well-being. And when I told Amanda she wouldn't call unless it was important… I just knew it. I could also tell she was annoyed with me for the way I answered her call. That Jamaican accent is a dead giveaway. She only puts it on in times of stress or when she's pissed at me.

"What is it?" I asked.

"There's someone here to see you, is what it is," she replied.

"A new client?" I asked. "Surely you don't need me for—"

"It's kinda complicated, Harry," she said, cutting me off.

"You can do complicated," I said.

"Dat, I can," she said. "But this is one of those t'ings only you can handle."

"So, what's it about?" I asked. "Why the secrecy?"

I heard her huff. Then she said, "She says it's personal."

"Personal?" I said, frowning. "What the hell?"

This time I heard her sigh before she said, "She says her name is Betty Markham, but you would know her as Betty Archer, and she wants to talk to you about her brother. Harry, she won't take no for an answer."

"Betty Archer?" I said, stunned. "David's sister?"

I could hear her talking to someone, presumably the client.

"Yes, that's right," Jacque said. "David Archer's sister. She also said you'd know all about it. What's going on, Harry?"

"I…" I hesitated, glanced at Amanda, who was watching me closely. "It's complicated, Jacque," I said. "Not something I can explain over the phone. Tell her I'll be there as soon as I can. I need to take Amanda and Jade home. It could take me an hour, depending on the traffic." I ended the call.

"We can take the limo service," Amanda said. A little testily, I thought.

I sighed and shook my head. "That might be for the best," I said. "I'm sorry, Amanda. My plan was to take the rest of the day off and spend it with you and Jade. But this…"

"What is it, Harry?" she asked.

Again, I shook my head. I also shrugged, then said, "As I told Jacque, it's complicated. It's something that happened many years ago when I was a young cop. My first case as lead detective, a murder case. I solved it quickly. Perhaps too quickly. I don't know. The guy—David Archer—swore he was innocent. But don't they all? But… Amanda, there was something about it; something I've never been able to put my finger on that bugged me. To this day, I can't tell you what it is. And now… his sister has turned up. She's at the office and insisting she talk with me."

"Then you should go," Amanda said. "We'll be fine. I'll call the limo service since they'll have a car seat. No problem. You go, and Jade and I will have some of that home-made Italian cream cake. Okay?"

I looked at her and smiled. "I'm sorry. You want me to call one for you?"

"Er… no!" she said, taking out her phone. "I'm quite capable of doing it all by myself."

I waited while she made the call, then said, "I'll see you in the cab before I leave."

She put the phone down, looked at me, and made a face.

I shook my head. After the events of the past several years, there was no way I was going to leave her until I'd seen her safely on her way.

"Two orders of Italian cream cake," she told the hovering waiter, "and a refill for our daughter."

3

FIFTEEN MINUTES LATER, WE WALKED OUT INTO THE SUNLIGHT where the SUV was waiting. Amanda helped Jade into the rear seat and buckled her in, then she turned to me and said, "Are you alright, Harry? You look as if you've been kicked in the gut."

I looked at her for a moment, then said, "I'm not sure. Betty Archer. Whew!"

She stared at me, her beautiful green eyes wide.

My wife is a beautiful, caring woman. We've been married a little over eight years. And I love her dearly, but it hasn't always been that way. There was a time when, lovely as she is, I couldn't stand the sight of her. Back then, she was an anchor at Channel 7 TV and a successful investigative reporter; she still is. In 2013, she did an on-air profile of me that wasn't exactly flattering. It was, in fact, an unfair attack on me personally and my agency in general. And then she had the temerity to demand an interview which, of course, I refused to grant. I swore she'd never get the chance to do it again. Funny how times and situations change. Long story short, three days later she stormed into my office, right past Jacque, sat down and refused to budge until I talked to her. Well, one thing led to another, and here we are.

"It's that bad?" she asked.

I shrugged. "I'm not sure," I repeated. "Possibly. I won't know until I talk to her, but—" I cut myself off, then said, "I'll tell you all about it, tonight. In the meantime, take Jade home. I'll be as quick as I can."

And, of course, as quick as I can, turned out to be a couple of hours.

I watched my wife and daughter leave, then went to my car, called Jacque, and told her I was on my way, then I made a left onto Shallowford Road, then another onto I-75 and then took Highway 153 to Riverside Drive where my offices are located.

Twenty minutes later, I walked into my outer office to find Jacque waiting for me.

"I gave her coffee and put her in your office," she said. "I hope you don't mind."

I shook my head and said, "I think you'd better join me. It could become… confrontational."

"Oh, I believe you," she replied. "She's wound tighter than an angry rattlesnake. Whatever did you do to her?"

"Geez," I said as I reached for my office doorknob. "Just what I need. An encouraging word." I paused, my hand on the knob, then said, "I put her brother away for life."

"And that would do it," Jacque said, grinning. "Lead on, boss."

"Don't call me that," I said as I turned the knob and pushed the door open.

She was sitting in one of the two chairs in front of my desk, coffee in hand, but she jumped to her feet and turned to face me. It was like seeing a ghost.

Betty Markham. Betty Archer, as she'd been known, had aged beyond her forty years. She'd been a pretty nineteen-year-old brunette when I first met her twenty-one years ago. Now… she looked every minute of fifty. The once full face had thinned and was heavily lined. The soft brown eyes had hardened. She still had her figure but was dressed to fit her mood. She was wearing a dark brown business suit over a tan satin top; the skirt cut an inch above the knee.

"Mrs. Markham," I said as I stepped forward, my hand extended.

She looked at it, ignored it, locked eyes with me and said, "He didn't do it!"

I nodded slowly, then said, "Why don't we sit down and talk about it? You've met my business partner, Jacque Hale? She'll be joining us."

She looked at Jacque and nodded. Jacque smiled at her.

"Let's sit over there," I said, nodding at the coffee table flanked by twin couches. "It's more comfortable. Would you like more coffee?"

"Oh, do stop blathering, Harry," she said as she stepped over to the righthand couch and sat down, her hands clasped together in her lap. She looked up at Jacque and said, "No. No more coffee. Thank you."

Jacque and I sat down on the couch opposite, and, for a moment, we sat and stared at each other across the no-man's-land of the coffee table.

"How are you, Betty?" I asked, finally, more to break the ice than to know the answer. "It's been… a long time."

"I'm fine," she replied. "Twenty-one years," she said in a voice as hard as flint. "Twenty-one long years. And you? You look well enough. You should see David. He looks seventy. He didn't do it, Harry. He didn't kill Elizabeth Reynolds. You screwed up. And David's been locked up for twenty-one frickin' years."

I took a deep breath, looked down at the table, then again at her and said, "The evidence—"

"The evidence?" she snorted, cutting me off. "There was no evidence. Just the word of a drunk and a halfwit—"

"His DNA was found at the scene—"

"So was that of a dozen or so men," she retorted. "She was a high-class hooker, for Pete's sake. You," she said, emphasizing the word, "didn't bother to follow up. You," she said again emphasizing the word, "had your prime suspect, and you didn't follow any other lines of inquiry. You hung it on David. And he was stupid enough to let you."

"He didn't have an alibi, Betty," I replied. "He refused to talk. He refused to take the stand. A jury of his peers found him guilty. I just—"

"I've followed your career," she snapped, cutting me off for the fourth time. "You're a good detective, Harry Starke. Some would say you're a brilliant detective. So what happened? Have you never questioned yourself? It was your first case, wasn't it?" And she stared at me; an unblinking, lingering stare.

And I felt… Uncomfortable is not the word for it. The truth was, I'd questioned myself. My gut had been screaming at me for years, telling me something was wrong. Was I sure David Archer had killed Elizabeth Reynolds that night? At the time, yes, I was. His DNA was indeed found at the scene. Two eyewitnesses put him there. And he had no alibi. But… And thereby hangs the tale!

The ring! I thought and inwardly shook my head.

She continued to stare at me. I felt Jacque stir beside me, and I was sure she was feeling as uncomfortable as I was.

"You have to make it right," Betty said, finally. "You have to find the real killer."

"I—"

"No!" she snapped. "Don't even go there, Harry Starke. You owe it to him. You put him away. You get him out."

I took a deep breath and shook my head. "There's nothing I can do, Betty," I said, quietly. "I'm sorry."

She put her hand inside her coat, took out an envelope, and tossed it onto the coffee table.

"What's that?" I asked.

"Read it," she snapped.

I leaned forward and picked it up. The envelope was addressed to her. I looked at her, frowning.

"Go ahead," she said. "Read it."

I opened the envelope, took out the two sheets of paper, and looked at the hand-written missive. It was addressed to me. I read it, looked up at Betty, read it again, then handed it to Jacque for her to read. Then I crossed my arms, leaned back, and slowly nodded my head.

David Archer had an alibi for the night of the murder.

And then there's that damn ring, I thought.

One of Mike Willis's techs had found a diamond ring at the scene of the crime. We never found out who it belonged to. It wasn't Elizabeth's, or her mother's, her friends had never seen it before, and it was too big for her, anyway. It didn't belong to David's wife; it was too big for her, too. He didn't have a girlfriend and was adamant that he'd never seen it before. That ring had always bugged me. It made no sense.

Elizabeth Reynolds was… Well, I suppose you could call her a socialite. She came from a good home. Her parents were well off. She was well known among Chattanooga's upper set. She was also a thousand dollar a night escort. David was a mechanic at one of the dealerships on the motor mile. Their relationship was close but platonic; this also according to David. He maintained he'd never used her services, nor had he ever been intimate with her. "They were just friends."

Betty was right. It was, indeed, my first case as lead detective. I was twenty-eight, gung-ho, and ready to make a name for myself. It was a simple enough case. David Archer was the only suspect. We played it out that David was a scorned lover. Elizabeth rejected his advances. He lost it and strangled her to death. We had his DNA at the scene and two eyewitnesses who put him there less than thirty minutes before she died. Simple!

But what if it wasn't?

Not only did David not provide an alibi, but he refused to talk at all. Now, according to the letter, after more than twenty years, he was offering an alibi. A good one.

I looked at Jacque. She gave me the slightest shrug, then nodded.

"I was nineteen when Elizabeth died," Betty said. "David was twenty-six—"

"I remember your testimony, Betty," I said, interrupting her. "Nothing's changed, other than this letter. I—"

"If you'll let me finish, please," she snapped, angrily interrupting me.

I nodded, and she continued, "David was a quiet young man, but I remember he'd started going out late at night and not returning until the morning. This was the part of his life you couldn't account for. It's the reason you arrested him, that and the two clowns, the so-called eyewitnesses, you were able to find. One was an alcoholic, the other a manic-depressive paranoiac. Did it never occur to you they might have gotten their days mixed up?"

She paused, staring at me, her eyebrows raised in question. I pursed my lips and slowly shook my head. "They were quite adamant," I said.

She huffed, closed her eyes for a moment, then continued, "David would never talk to me about that night. All he would say was that he didn't kill her, and I believed him. He's my brother. Why wouldn't I? I knew him better than anyone. It wasn't until our parents passed away—Mom died in 2016, Dad in 2021—that David told me he was seeing someone and that he had been for years. I didn't think much of it. Not until I received that letter from him." She nodded at Jacque, who was still holding it.

"As you see," she continued, "he says he was seeing a woman named MaryAnn Williams; and he still is. I know MaryAnn. She's three years older than David. She was twenty-nine, and she was married, and so was he. I didn't even know he knew her. He never mentioned her to me, or to anyone else, as far as I know."

"So I went to see him. Last week. Three days after I received that." Again, she nodded toward Jacque. "He told me he met her when he fixed her car and that it was love at first sight, for both of them. However, MaryAnn has two children and didn't want to leave them or break up the family, but they met several times, for coffee, and such, but then something happened between them, and they began seeing each other at night when her husband was at home watching the kids. Not often. Once or twice a month. Sometimes just once a month. Girl's night out was what she told her husband. It was one of those nights that Elizabeth was killed. David was with MaryAnn. Yes, he'd gone to see Elizabeth earlier. But he was with MaryAnn when she died."

"That's quite a story," I said, only half-skeptically. "And it's convenient. How can you be sure David was with MaryAnn that night?"

She pointed to the letter and said, "Second to last paragraph!"

I took the letter from Jacque and re-read the paragraph.

Elizabeth called me. She said she was frightened and needed to talk to me. I went to her place. She was in tears. She said she had an appointment with a client, a man who liked rough sex. She'd seen him several times before. She said he liked to choke her, and he hurt her. She'd called him and told him she wasn't feeling well and needed to cancel the appointment, but he got angry and told her he needed to see her and would be there at eight as scheduled. So I waited, but he didn't show up. I waited till eight-thirty and then left and went to meet MaryAnn. I called Eliz-

abeth when I got there to make sure she was okay. He still hadn't turned up, and it was almost nine o'clock. MaryAnn was kind of pissed because I took so long. She didn't have much time. She can vouch for me. I was with her when Liz was murdered.

I slowly refolded the letter and then sat there for a moment in silence, thinking, then I looked up at Betty and said, "Why now?"

"David was in love with her," she replied. "He still is. He refused to drag her name through the mud. Nor did he want to break up her family."

"You didn't answer the question," I said. "Why now?"

She shrugged. "MaryAnn's husband found out that she was seeing him," she said. "He divorced her. It was finalized three months ago. She persuaded David to talk. He sent me that letter. David and MaryAnn are together now… Well, as together as they can be, considering where he is."

She stared at me for a long moment, then said, "The medical examiner put the time of death between nine-thirty and ten-thirty that evening. He was with MaryAnn. You need to fix this, Harry. I can pay." She looked at her watch and then rose to her feet. Jacque and I also stood.

She handed me a business card and said, "I'll expect to hear from you soon. Send me your bill."

And with that, she turned and walked out the door.

"Wow," Jacque said. "That was something. You want to talk about it?"

"No!" I stated. "Not tonight, anyway. I need to go home. Do me a favor. Have Tim find this MaryAnn Williams. I want a complete rundown on her and her ex-husband."

"So, you're going to take the case, then?"

"I didn't say that," I replied. "I'll see you here tomorrow morning, around nine. We'll talk then."

4

It was after six-thirty when I arrived home that Friday afternoon to find Amanda waiting for me, and she wasn't in the best of moods. Broken promises will do that to her, and I was guilty of breaking my promise to spend that afternoon with her and Jade.

"So," she said as I poured myself a good two fingers of Laphroaig, "I'm waiting."

I turned to face her, took a sip of my drink, tilted my head a little to one side and said, "Later, when Jade is in bed and I've had a chance to unwind."

She nodded, turned away, put on a mitt, went to the oven, took out a plate and set it on the kitchen table.

"Lasagna," she said. "It's probably ruined by now."

I nodded and sat down at the table.

"I'm sorry," I said. "It was personal, unavoidable."

She gifted me with a tight smile. "I know," she said. "You don't have to apologize. Would you like something to drink other than that?" She nodded at the glass in my hand.

"Some tea," I replied, "but I can get it."

"Of course you can," she said as she went to the fridge.

She returned with a pitcher and a glass full of iced tea, then said, "I'll have Maria put Jade to bed, then we can talk. You go ahead and eat."

The lasagna was homemade, and it wasn't spoiled. And though I know I enjoyed every bite, I don't really remember eating it. What I do remember is reliving the events of 2001.

I must have sat there staring at my empty plate for a good twenty minutes before Amanda returned and asked me if I was finished.

I looked up at her and nodded.

"Jade's in bed," she said, "and Maria left a few minutes ago. So, if you want, you can go up and say goodnight."

I got up from the table, took my plate and glass to the sink, then turned to her and said, "Okay, I'll be just a minute."

Jade was feisty and in no mood to sleep. She insisted I read her a story and, though I wasn't in the mood for it, I made the effort and read *The Ugly Duckling*; she was asleep in minutes.

Amanda was in the living room with the TV on and a glass of white wine on the coffee table in front of her.

She looked up at me as I entered the room, reached for the remote, and paused the TV.

I sat down on the couch next to her, took her hand and said, "I'm sorry."

"It's okay," she replied. "D'you want to tell me about it?"

I nodded, thought for a minute, then began, "It was in July 2001. It was my first case as lead detective. Elizabeth Reynolds was found strangled to death in her apartment. It was one of those 'first forty-eight' things." I made quotes with my fingers. "I had a young fella, David Archer, for it. It was a slam dunk. At least I thought it was, until today, when his sister showed up at my office. I put him away for life. He's been locked up for twenty-one years. If he didn't do it, that's on me. I was so sure, but now…" I shook my head.

"Hmm, July 2001," she said, thoughtfully. "I was just out of Columbia. I didn't start at Channel 7 until September." She made a face and shrugged. "It was before my time."

"I was sure it was him," I said, "but there was something."

"Something?" she asked, frowning. "What d'you mean?"

"I don't know," I replied. "I always felt there was something I was missing. Maybe I didn't take enough time." I shook my head, then continued, "Archer grew up next door to Reynolds. He claimed they'd been friends since they were kids, and the evidence confirmed it, but I believed they were more than just friends. She was an escort. She was living in an apartment on the Southside. His DNA was found in the apartment, and two eyewitnesses put him in the building only thirty minutes before she died. He was also known to have a violent temper, as his ex-wife, Sara, with whom he had a volatile relationship, was only too happy to testify. And he had no alibi. It was open and shut, except…"

She waited for me to continue and when I didn't, she said, "Except for…"

"We found a ring," I said. "A diamond ring, a woman's Tiffany engagement ring, on the carpet near the door. It wasn't Elizabeth's, that was obvious. It was two sizes too big. And it didn't belong to David or his wife. We ran DNA on it, but we didn't get a match. Its presence at the scene was never explained."

"And you had no other suspects?" Amanda asked.

I shook my head.

She looked at me skeptically. "Did you look for any?"

Again, I slowly shook my head.

"Why not?" she asked.

"I told you," I replied. "It was a gimme, a one-foot putt. I had him dead to rights. He refused to talk. He had no defense. What was I supposed to do?"

"I think the words you're looking for are due diligence," she replied caustically. "What are you going to do?"

"I haven't decided yet," I said.

"Oh, don't give me that, Harry," she replied. "I know you better than you know yourself. When are you going to talk to him, to Archer?"

I smiled at her. It was true. She did know me, and she was right, but it wasn't until that moment I realized it myself.

Had I taken the route of least resistance? I was already thinking that perhaps I had. But what to do about it? That was the question I was struggling with.

"One day next week, I suppose," I replied.

"That's my boy," she said and leaned in and kissed me. It was one of those kisses that sent shivers down my spine: light, lingering, full of promise.

We talked for several minutes more, marking time, I guess, then went up to bed for what was supposed to be an early night. The promise? She kept it, of course. Amanda always keeps her promises.

5

NEEDLESS TO SAY, I DIDN'T SLEEP WELL THAT NIGHT. AMANDA, as always, slept like a log. Me? I tossed and turned, slept fitfully, watched the clock until, finally, I'd had enough. I slipped quietly out of bed, donned a pair of swim shorts, and went out to the pool. It was almost five-thirty.

I swam fifty laps, got out of the water, toweled myself off, then went into the kitchen and made coffee. I poured myself a cup and took it out onto the patio.

It was still dark and would be for at least another hour. I sat down on the low wall that bounds the pool and patio and watched the lights of the awakening city below.

I was in a pensive mood. I'd had David Archer on my mind most of the night, and the six hours tossing and turning had done nothing to lighten my mood.

I sipped my coffee and stared unseeing at the city lights, reliving those forty-eight hours all those years ago. Could I have done things differently? Perhaps. We certainly closed it out quickly. Let me put it this way: had it been today, I most definitely would have done it differently.

But hindsight is always twenty-twenty, right?

I must have been out there on the patio wall for almost an hour when I felt a pair of warm hands on my bare shoulders.

"Hey, you," I said without turning to look at her. "Come and sit with me and watch the sunrise."

"Would you like some more coffee?" Amanda asked.

I shook my head. "No, not right now," I replied. "Maybe later."

She sat down beside me and swung her legs around and over the wall so she was sitting beside me. She took my hand in both of hers and squeezed it.

"Rough night?" she asked.

"Did I bother you?"

"I always know when you have a rough night, but no, not really."

I smiled at her and said, "You'd never know it, the way you were snoring."

She dropped my hand like it was a hot coal. "I do not snore," she retorted.

"It's cute," I said, grinning.

She slapped my leg. "I don't snore, Harry," she repeated, then said, "It's David Archer, isn't it?"

I nodded, staring down at the silvery ribbon of the Tennessee River.

"I think I may have screwed up," I said. "And if I did, I've cost that man a half a lifetime behind bars. I don't know if he's innocent or not. If he is, I don't know if I can put it right, and even if I can, nothing can replace the years he's lost."

She took my hand again, laid her head on my shoulder, and said, "It's not your fault, Harry. He refused to give you his alibi. That's on him. Not you."

I sighed and shook my head.

"Will you look at that sky?" she said. "Is that not the most beautiful thing you've ever seen?"

The sun was rising in a blaze of glory over the Sequoyah Nuclear Plant on the far horizon. She was only half right, but it was beautiful.

I turned to look at her. Her face was bathed in the golden glow of the dawn. "Not by a long shot," I said. "The most beautiful thing I've ever seen is sitting right next to me."

"Nice one," she said, then leaned in close and kissed me. "I love you so much, Harry Starke."

IT WAS a little before nine when I arrived at my offices that Saturday morning to find Jacque, along with TJ and Tim, already there waiting for me. Heather was away visiting family in Baltimore for a few days.

"You want coffee?" Jacque asked as we walked to the elevator.

"That would be nice," I said.

"Me, too," TJ said.

"And me," Tim added.

"Go on up, Harry," Jacque said. "We'll join you in a minute."

My office is… big. It occupies almost a third of the second floor. It's not as comfortable as the one I had on Georgia before it was bombed by Lester "Shady" Tree, but it offers a quiet refuge from the day-to-day grind.

I opened the door and walked inside. The lights, sensing my presence, came on automatically as I went to my desk and sat down.

I sat there for a moment, ruminating, then tapped the keyboard and brought up the lock screen. Barely had I done so when the door opened, and Jacque stepped inside, followed by TJ and Tim.

"Let's do the couches," I said, rising to my feet. "It's Saturday, so there's no need for formality."

"Formality?" Jacque asked as she set a large mug of black coffee down on the coffee table. "I don't recall that ever being a priority around here."

"Me neither," Tim said, grinning as he unloaded his coffee, laptop and iPhone onto the table and parked himself on the edge of the couch farthest from the door. I sat on the couch opposite him. Jacque sat next to me.

TJ, as always stoically silent, sat down next to Tim and leaned back, coffee in hand.

TJ Bron is one of those people you read about but rarely meet. He's an anomaly. He was homeless, living on the streets, and in sad shape when Kate Gazzara brought him to me. He'd discovered the body of a young woman in a back alley. Kate was the investigating officer, and she saw something in him nobody else did, so she brought him to me. He had little to say, as usual, but I had Tim run his background and it turned out he was a highly decorated Marine, a Vietnam vet—two tours, 1968 and 1972. He was also an accountant and it just so happened… Well, to cut to the chase, I hired him. Jacque found him an apartment, and the rest is, as they say, history. Oh, and since I hired him, he's saved my life… twice.

"So," I said, after taking a sip of my coffee. "You're probably wondering what this is about."

"Jacque sort of filled us in while we were waiting for you," Tim said.

I nodded. "She doesn't know the half of it," I said, and proceeded to tell the story of my investigation of the Elizabeth Reynolds murder.

"What Jacque doesn't know," I added, "is that I was under a lot of pressure to close it out quickly. As I said, we had what we needed to convict Archer. He refused to talk and so I charged him and basically washed my hands of it."

"What do you mean you were under a lot of pressure?" TJ asked.

"My boss at the time was Sergeant Tom Miller," I replied. "Henry Finkle, a lieutenant at the time, was putting pressure on Tom to convict Archer. Tom, in turn, put pressure on me. I didn't think too much about it at the time. I was basically a rookie detective, so I went along with it. Even so, I felt there was something off about it. That diamond ring bugged the hell out of me. It was expensive; the stone was almost two karats." I shook my head. "It was my first case—no excuses—and, on thinking back, I didn't know what the hell I was doing. It was rushed, all done in the first forty-eight hours. I should have done more. We didn't interview Reynolds' clients. We didn't interview her friends, and Betty Markham was right about the two eyewitnesses. They could have gotten their days mixed up."

"But why would he take a life sentence to protect his lover?" Jacque asked. "And why would she let him? Why didn't she come forward? She can't think much of him. It makes no sense. And he's still seeing her? Really?"

"It does seem a little radical, I agree," I said, "but there's nothing so strange as folk, so they say, and love is a mighty powerful endorphin."

"Henry Finkle," TJ said, thoughtfully. "I always thought there was something off about that son of a bitch. Sneaky little bastard."

"Tiny was… He was…" I couldn't find the words I needed to describe him without resorting to profanity, and that was something I rarely did, and especially not in front of Jacque. "Let's just say he knows the right people and leave it at that."

"Wasn't he demoted?" Tim asked.

I nodded. "He was. For sexual harassment."

"Wasn't it Kate that brought him down?" Jacque asked.

"It was," I replied, "though she's never really talked about it."

"D'you think…?" Tim didn't finish the question, but I knew what he was getting at.

I shook my head. "You're asking me if Henry could have killed Elizabeth?" I asked. "Anyone can kill, given the right circumstances, including Henry, but I doubt he did it. Though he might have been a client, and if he was, and if he was about to be outed… Then all bets are off."

"You said he was applying pressure," Jacque said. "Why would he do that unless he had a good reason, a personal reason?"

"Pressure from higher up," I said. "Pressure to get a conviction. It happens all the time. It was one of the reasons I got out of there. That and the politics.

"Elizabeth Reynolds was a high-end escort," I said. "A fact that was glossed over. She had a lot of clients, most of them in high places. I think David Archer was the convenient fall guy, especially since he was thought to be the last person to see her alive. The time of death was established as between nine and ten-thirty. If he was where he says he was, he didn't do it."

"So, what's the plan?" Jacque asked. "Are you going to take it?"

I thought for a moment. It was a question I'd been asking myself ever since Betty Markham had left my office. I turned and looked at Jacque. She locked eyes with me, raised her eyebrows, and smiled.

I shrugged.

"If I know you, Harry Starke," she said, the Jamaican accent strong in her voice, "you don't get to d'bottom of it, you not gonna be able to live with y'self. I t'ink you better do it."

And there it was. That was all the encouragement I needed.

"Let's do it," I said.

Tim grinned and nodded enthusiastically.

"When do I get to interview Henry Finkle?" TJ asked.

"We'll do that together," I said. "This thing happened twenty-one years ago, so the first thing we have to do is gather as much information as we can. Tim, that's your job. I want you to find the two eyewitnesses: Lucas James and Joey Breen. He was a custodian at Reynolds' apartment building. He was a little slow, a conspiracy theorist, paranoid. Reynolds also had a close friend; Shirley…" I wrinkled my brow. "Walker? Yeah, that's it. Shirley Walker. She was an escort, too. We need to find her. Maybe she can provide us with some names." I took a sip of my coffee while I thought about my next steps.

"I need to talk to Archer and MaryAnn. Jacque, you and I will do that. Make an appointment to visit the prison for one day next week, Tuesday or Wednesday, if you can. We'll see MaryAnn at her convenience, but the sooner the better. So… we have the makings of a plan. Take the rest of the weekend off. We'll get to work first thing Monday morning—"

"Whoa!" Jacque exclaimed. "What about our current cases? We can't just slough them off."

"And we won't," I said. "We'll take Monday, Tuesday, and Wednesday, see what comes of it, then talk again. In the meantime, I'll get hold of Kate and see if she can find the Archer file."

Jacque made a face, then said, "What about Heather?"

"When's she due back?" I asked.

"Monday, so she said."

"Perfect," I said. "We'll bring her up to speed and… Look, if this thing takes off, we may have to set some things aside, but that's okay. We're up to date with most of our cases, are we not?" I looked at TJ, then at Tim. Both nodded.

"That's it then," I said. "We'll meet in the conference room on Monday morning at eight sharp. Now go. Enjoy your weekend. Yeah, you, too, Jacque. No arguments."

6

I ARRIVED HOME THAT AFTERNOON AT A LITTLE AFTER TWELVE-thirty. It was another beautiful day with temperatures in the mid-seventies. Jade was outside on the patio with Maria. Amanda was in the kitchen preparing a late lunch: a rosemary ham salad.

"Well?" she asked as I went to the fridge for a beer. "How did it go?"

"Pretty much as I expected," I said, taking a bottle opener from the drawer. "We start work on Monday."

I removed the top from the bottle of Blue Moon, dropped it into the trash, and sat down at the table.

"And?" she asked.

"And we start work on Monday," I repeated. "There's not much we can do until we've gathered information. I have Tim chasing down witnesses and contacts, and…" I checked my watch, "I need to call Kate. D'you mind?"

She shook her head. "Of course not." And she sat down at the table opposite me.

I grinned at her. "I wasn't going to do it right away," I said, "but since you're sitting there looking at me all wide eyed and curious, here goes."

I took my phone from my pocket and hit the speed dial for Kate's cell phone. She answered almost immediately.

"Harry? What's up? I would have thought you'd be out on the golf course."

"Not today," I replied. "Look, I need a favor. I need access to an old file. One of mine. How about it?"

She was silent for a moment, then said, "And… why would you want to do that?"

"It's a long story, Kate," I said. "Let's just say I have some unfinished business to deal with. I'll explain when I see you."

"Which file, Harry?" she asked, dryly.

"The David Archer file."

I could imagine her frowning. "I don't remember that one. When was it?" she asked.

"It was my first case as lead detective, July 2001."

"Geez," she said, "I was just a rookie. Okay. I was about to leave for the weekend, but I'll see what I can do," she said. "You want me to drop it by?"

"That would be nice," I said. "We have beer and wine. Bring Samson. Jade loves him."

"If I can find it," she said. "I'll call you."

"Thanks," I said and hung up.

I took a sip of my beer and spent the next twenty minutes, or so, filling Amanda in on my plan, such as it was, then stood up and grabbed another beer.

"I would have thought we'd have heard from her by now," I said, sitting down again.

"Harry, it hasn't been thirty minutes," Amanda said. "Give her a chance."

I nodded. "Come on," I said. "Let's go out on the patio. This weather's not going to last much longer." And we did.

It was two o'clock when Kate arrived with Samson. She parked in the driveway and turned him loose. He came bounding around the house and went straight to Jade and licked her face. She squealed and giggled and squealed some more. Then he turned away and ran to Amanda, who didn't squeal but did make a fuss of him. Kate followed him in, carrying a banker's box.

"There," she said, plonking it down on the table. "It's kinda light, don't you think?"

"Don't you start," I said, taking the top off the box and peering inside. It was indeed kinda light.

Kate made nice with Amanda, Jade and Maria, then went inside to get a beer. She returned a few moments later, bottle in hand, and sat down at the table.

"So," she said. "What's it about, Harry? Am I going to lose my job over this, or what?"

"I wouldn't have thought so," I replied. "You ran it by the chief?"

She nodded. "He told me to tell you to be careful."

"Well he would, wouldn't he?" I said. "He was an assistant chief at the time. I was twenty-eight. It was July 12, 2001. I'd made detective eight months earlier in December 2000. I was excited. Tom Miller was my immediate boss. Henry Finkle was his boss. It was supposed to be a simple, open-and-shut case. And it was, or so I thought. They wanted a quick result. I gave them one. I closed it in the first forty-eight, much to everyone's delight… All except Johnston. He took me to one side and asked me if I was sure." I shrugged. "What was I supposed to say? I told him I was, but even as I said it, my gut was telling me something else."

"So why didn't you go with your gut?" Amanda asked. "You always do!"

I was silent for a moment, took the murder book out of the box, opened it and stared at the photo of Elizabeth Reynolds.

"It wasn't as simple as that," I said, finally. "It was the first time I'd ever felt anything like that. I didn't know what it meant. It was something I had to learn. I had to learn to trust it. Back then…" I shrugged. "And there was the ring," I continued. "I told you about that," I said to Amanda, and then to Kate I said, "We found a Tiffany engagement ring at the scene. It didn't belong to the victim, and it didn't belong to Archer. We never found out who it belonged to, but it bothered me; it still does."

Kate made a face. "So, after all this time, you've decided to listen to your gut?" she said. "How sure are you Archer is innocent?"

I thought for a minute, then replied, "I'm not sure at all. He's claiming he has an alibi. If he does, and it's good…" I shook my head. "His lover's agreed to come forward. But, as you well know, it's never that easy. It's just her word. Maybe it's good. And even if it is, would three appeal court judges believe it? I'm not sure they would. They'd need more evidence than that."

"So, what are you going to do?" Kate asked.

I leaned forward after taking a pull from my beer. "I'm going to re-investigate it. I have to. If Archer is innocent, we need to fix it. I've suspended operations through Wednesday. We'll give it our best shot and then reevaluate."

Kate nodded. We both looked at Amanda. She smiled, nodded, and said, "What can I do to help?"

"I'm not sure," I said. "As I recall, there was very little media coverage. Maybe you could dig through Channel 7's archives and see what you can find."

She nodded. "I was planning on doing that, anyway. First thing Monday morning."

"I keep thinking about the way Tom Miller and Henry Finkle were in such a rush to close it out," I said.

"I never really knew Tom," Kate said, "but, as you both know, I know Henry all too well. It wouldn't surprise me if he was involved in some kind of cover-up. Not that that's what we have here, though, unless…"

"You know," I said, thoughtfully, "Finkle had little to say to me. It was Tom who put the pressure on." I paused for a second or two, thinking about those two days in general and Henry Finkle in particular.

"He and I never really got along," I said. "And Johnston, too. We had our moments. Maybe I should talk to him, too."

"They don't have to talk to you, Harry," Kate said, seriously. "You're not a cop anymore, and what you're about to do is create a lot of trouble for yourself. Finkle will come down on you hard."

I grinned at her. "It's been tried before," I said. "I can handle him. And so can you, as I recall."

"Yeah, well," she said. "That was a long time ago. Times have changed. He's not quite the nasty little creep he once was. And I steer well clear of him, anyway."

She rose to her feet. "I gotta go," she said. "I have a hot date. Dinner at Ruth's Chris and… Who knows?"

"Thomas Drews?" I asked, grinning, as I stood up.

"What d'you think?" she said. Then, "Keep a tight rein on him, Amanda. He's not as young as he was, but he's still driven by his impulses and that gut of his."

"Oh, don't you know it?" Amanda said. "Have a pleasant night, Kate. Talk to you soon?"

"You bet," Kate said, then turned to me and said, "Take it easy, Harry. I'll help if I can. You want me to keep the chief in the loop?"

"It couldn't hurt," I said. "Have a good rest of the weekend, Kate, and tell Thomas hello for me."

"I will," she said. "Call me if you need me." Then she looked around, spotted Samson on the far side of the pool, and said, "Say goodbye to Jade, Sammy."

Samson ran over to Jade and gave her a sloppy kiss that set her off giggling again. And they left.

Me? I sat down again and picked up my almost empty beer bottle. I held it up, looked at it, put it to my lips and downed what was left. It was warm, but it still tasted good.

The rest of the weekend went pretty much to plan. I played golf with my father on Sunday morning. We had lunch at the club, and Amanda cooked a roast for the evening meal.

It was relaxing. Well, it would have been had I not spent almost all of it thinking about David Archer and Elizabeth Reynolds, and the more I thought about it, the more convinced I became that there had been a gross miscarriage of justice.

And I knew I had to put it right.

7

It was ten minutes to eight that Monday morning when I walked into the conference room carrying the banker's box. Needless to say, they were all there ahead of me, except for Jacque, who'd met me at the door.

"Settle down, everyone," I said as I set the box down on the table. "I need to get some coffee, then we'll begin."

"No need for that," Jacque said, setting a large mug of steaming coffee down in front of me.

"Oh, thanks," I said and picked it up and took a sip. Had I been on my own, I would have sighed with pleasure. As it was, I set the mug down and said, "Good morning. I hope you all had a wonderful weekend, but now it's time to go to work."

I looked at Heather and said, "Heather, this is—"

"It's okay, Harry," she said, cutting me off. "I came in early. Jacque brought me up to speed."

Heather Stillwell is my lead investigator. She's been with me almost from the beginning. She's in her mid-forties but looks much younger. She's five-eight, has short brown hair, an oval face, brown eyes, and is in better shape than anyone I know, except for TJ. She works out every morning, teaches self-defense to women in her spare time, and is an expert shot. Before she came to work for me, she spent the first two years of her law enforcement career as a street cop in Atlanta until she was recruited by the Georgia Bureau of Investigation. I'd met her several times during my investigations. I liked her. She was a good cop.

Then, she called me. She asked if I was needing any help. It was right around the time things were beginning to move for my agency. We were busy. I hadn't had a day off in months. We talked. I liked what I heard, so I hired her. She never told me why she wanted to leave the GBI, but I suspect it was a lifestyle thing. Heather's gay, and quite open about it. She's been with me a long time and I trust her implicitly.

"You jailed an innocent man," she said, "and we have to clean up the mess?"

"I wouldn't have put it quite like that," I said, "but… essentially, yes."

I looked around the table. "So, this is how I see it," I said. "Right now, we need information, and we can start with this." I tapped the box with a finger. "This is the case file. It's pretty slim: my fault, I'm afraid. Heather. I want you to go through it this morning. I've already been through it, but we need a second pair of experienced eyes."

"Tim—"

"Er, yeah," he said, interrupting me. "I found the two eyewitnesses. Lucas James is dead. He died of a fentanyl overdose. Joey Breen is in a nursing home on Ringgold Road. I also found Shirley Walker. She's—"

"When did you do all this, Tim?" I asked, cutting him off.

He frowned, pursed his lips, pushed his glasses further up the bridge of his nose with the tip of his finger, then said, hesitantly, "I… err… Yesterday?"

"Are you asking me?" I said. "Didn't I tell you to go home and take the weekend off?"

"Well, I did," he said. "Go home." He shrugged, then continued, "I was bored. I had nothing to do. Don't you hate that, having nothing to do? I do, so I just did it." Again, he poked at his glasses. "So, I found Shirley Walker. You want to know where?"

"Tell me more about her, and then tell me where she is now," I said, frowning, realizing I'd just let Tim loose.

"She was one of Elizabeth Reynolds' contemporaries. She was an escort. One of her friends, maybe. Websites back then weren't what they are today, but there were a few. There was no social media. Myspace was the first, but it didn't launch until August 2003. Hookers advertised in the yellow pages—which is where I found Shirley and Elizabeth, by the way, but it wasn't easy because…" He caught my look, and said, "Oh, yeah. Okay. So, a few enterprising ones created primitive, individual websites. All of that means it's hard to track them down. I'm still searching, but so far Shirley is all I've come up with."

I took a deep breath, glared at him, and shook my head. I should have known better. It was typical of him.

So I nodded and said, "Good job, Tim, as always. Thank you. I've found another name for you: Amy Murphy. Apparently, she was Elizabeth Reynolds' closest friend. She was also an escort. I interviewed her back in the day, but she wasn't talking. Find her. We need to talk to her again."

"You got it, boss."

I frowned at him. He got the message. "Sorry, Harry!"

I nodded. "That's better," I said, then turned to Jacque and said, "See if you can make an appointment for me to see Archer. In the meantime," I looked at TJ, "you and I will go talk to the witness, Joey, then Shirley Walker."

TJ nodded, then said, "How about Henry Finkle?"

I grinned at him and said, "All in good time, TJ. All in good time.

"Heather," I said. "As soon as Tim finds the Murphy woman, I want you to interview her. We need names. That's on you and TJ." I looked at him. He nodded.

"I want to know who Elizabeth's friends were," I said. "I want to know who her clients were. I want the name of anyone who might have had a grudge against her. I want motives. I want means, and I want opportunity. And I want it all by Wednesday afternoon at four so we can reevaluate. Questions?"

"What do you want me to do?" Jacque asked.

"For now, I need that appointment," I replied. "That done, I want you to coordinate with Tim. Prioritize the names as they come in. If all goes well, TJ and I will be back by lunchtime. That okay?"

She nodded, hesitated, then said, "I don't like closing down for three days. I can put Lucy on the front desk, but I think we should consider hiring another investigator. It's not been easy since Bob Ryan left."

I nodded slowly, digesting what she'd said, already knowing she was right.

"You've been thinking about this for a while, haven't you?" I asked.

She nodded. I looked around the table. It was obvious the rest of my team was in agreement.

"Any ideas?" I asked Jacque.

"One or two," she replied. "You want me to put out some feelers, set up some interviews?"

I thought for a moment, then nodded and said, "Yes, but leave the interviews until the end of the week. Maybe we can do a couple on Friday afternoon, depending on how this week goes."

I stood up, looked around the table, and said, "Let's get to it. Tim, I need those addresses. Send them to my phone, please. TJ, grab some coffee and let's get out of here."

8

We found Joey Breen in a low-end, subsidized retirement home—and I say "retirement home" with some serious reservations—on Ringgold Road. He was in a wheelchair next to a small round table in a large public area close to a floor-to-ceiling window with a view of a dusty, concrete backyard.

"Not the most inspiring view," I muttered to TJ as we crossed the room.

TJ didn't answer.

"Joey," I said, holding out my hand for him to shake.

"Who the hell are you?" he asked, ignoring my hand. "You look fa… fa… Do I know you?"

"Oh yeah, Joey. You know me," I said, pulling up a chair, nodding to TJ to do the same, and then I sat down in front of him, leaned forward, put my elbows on my knees, clasped my hands together in front of me, and locked eyes with him.

He'd aged. Not in a good way. His face was covered in liver spots. The backs of his hands crawled with thick, knotted veins. His jowls were sagging, as was his neck. His eyes, the palest blue, lacked sparkle. His hair, formerly brown as I remembered it, was dirty white and thinned to the point where I could see his liver-spotted skull.

"You're looking well, Joey," I lied. "Feel like talking?"

"I know you," he croaked. "You're that frickin' cop. Get the hell outta here. I got nothin' to say to you or any other cop."

"I'm not a cop anymore, Joey," I said. "And I feel much the same as you do."

He narrowed his eyes, tucked his chin into his sagging neck, stared at me, then said, "You got a taste?"

"Have I got something to drink, you mean?" I said. "You know better than that, Joey. Isn't that why you're here?"

"Aaah piss off," he winged. "This place? It's like a frickin' prison. Look at that view. Not even a frickin' pot plant. Miserable sons-a-bitches! What is it you want?"

"I want to talk to you about Elizabeth Reynolds," I said. "You remember her, right?"

"Yeah'do," his eyes lit up, and he almost smiled. "Lisbeth. Lovely girl. Shame what happened to her. Son of a bitch strangled the poor kid. They fried the bastard yet?"

"Archer?" I asked. "He's still in prison, if that's who you're talking about."

"Yeah, him," he said, then coughed violently without covering his mouth. I reacted instinctively and reared back in my chair.

He grinned at me, wickedly, and wiped his mouth on the sleeve of his jacket; and not for the first time, I could see.

"He shoulda gotten the chair," he half-croaked, half coughed. "What he done to that kid was criminal."

"You helped put him away, Joey," I said. "I take it you haven't changed your mind about anything."

"Huh?" he said, squinting at me. "What you talkin' about? Why would I change my mind? He done it. I saw him."

"You saw him?" I asked. "You saw him kill her?" I was

incredulous. That was not what he said when I interviewed him. Nor did he testify as such at Archer's trial.

"Nah!" he rasped. "Course not, but I saw him. He was there. Never saw no one else."

"Could you have gotten the time wrong?" I asked. "Could it have been earlier when you saw him?"

"What you tryin' t'do, asshole? You tryin' to get 'im off?" he asked. "No, sir! No frickin', sir. I was there. It was a Friday, the day 'Lizbeth got kilt. I got off at eight. He was still there when I left. I know what I know, and you ain't gonna make me say no different. So now you can get the hell outta here and leave me the hell alone."

"And you didn't see anyone else?" I persisted.

"Screw you," he croaked and burst out coughing again.

"Come on, Harry," TJ said. "You're not going to get anything more out of him."

"Screw you, too, you son-a-bitch," Joey muttered, wiping his mouth. "Who the hell are you, anyway?"

"How about her friends, Joey?" I asked, giving it one last try. "Did any of them visit her that afternoon or evening? How about clients?"

"That's enough, I think," a firm voice behind me said.

I looked around. The male nurse was the size of a house. Think Dwayne Johnson on steroids.

TJ looked up at him. Stood up and said, "We were just leaving, weren't we, Harry?"

I looked again at Joey. He had that same wicked grin on his lips.

I stood up.

"Have a nice day, cop," he rasped, then looked up at the nurse and said, "Get 'em outta here, Dell."

"That didn't go too well, did it?" TJ said, grinning, as we walked back to my car.

I grinned back at him and said, “Screw you, you son-a-bitch.”

He just shook his head, smiling, then said, “What now, chief?”

“Shirley Walker,” I said as I opened the car door.

9

Shirley Walker's address was an older, two-story home in the prestigious Stonehenge neighborhood in Ooltewah just to the north of the city.

It was almost noon when TJ and I stepped out of the car and up onto the front porch. The grounds were beautifully manicured. The paintwork appeared to be new. It was, as they say, an idyllic location and property.

"Not bad for a hooker," TJ said as I thumbed the doorbell button. "Looks like she's done well for herself."

The door opened before I could reply, and we were confronted by a tall and strikingly beautiful woman.

"Can I help you?" she asked.

"Shirley Walker?" I asked.

She frowned, then said, "No… I'm Shirley Castle. Who are you? What do you want?"

"My name's Harry Starke, Mrs. Castle. I'm a private investigator. This is my associate, TJ Bron. We're looking for Shirley Walker. That's you, isn't it?"

She stared at me for a moment, then stepped back. I thought

she was going to slam the door in our faces, but she didn't. Instead, she said, "You'd better come in."

She led us through the house to the kitchen, then turned and said, "You can sit down. Coffee? Tea? Water?"

"Nothing for me, thank you," I said as I sat down at the kitchen table.

She looked at TJ. He shook his head, pulled his notepad and pencil out, and sat down next to me.

"How did you find me?" she asked as she sat down opposite us.

"I have a gifted IT person," I replied.

She nodded but said nothing more. Instead, she stared at me, her eyes half-closed, her hands linked on top of the table.

She was indeed beautiful: five-nine or ten, natural blonde hair, startling blue eyes, unblemished skin and, as far as I could tell, not a gram of Botox anywhere. From Tim's report, I knew she was forty-six, which made her twenty-five when Reynolds was murdered.

"We're looking into the murder of Elizabeth Reynolds," I said. "I understand you were a friend of hers."

"You mean I was a hooker?" she replied, smiling.

"If that's how you want to put it," I said, locking eyes with her.

She clicked her tongue, looked down at the table, then at TJ, then at me. "I know who you are," she said. "You're the cop that put that Archer kid away, aren't you?"

"I am… I was," I replied. "I'm a private investigator now."

"And you think you've figured it out?" she said. "You think you made a mistake?" She smiled, then continued. "I never thought he did it. He was Liz's friend; probably the only real friend she had."

"Was he screwing her?" TJ asked, bluntly.

"Ah," she said, lightly, and leaned back in her chair and

folded her arms, "it speaks. No. He wasn't. They'd been friends since they were kids. He was like a brother to her."

I stared at her. There was something about this woman you couldn't help but like.

"I know what you're thinking," she said, smiling. "What's she doing here? How come she's not some old slag like all the rest of Lana's whores?"

"I—" I began.

But she interrupted me. "I was one of the lucky ones," she said. "I married one of my clients. You must know him. Chester Castle?"

Oh, yeah. I knew him. Castle was a high-power federal attorney working out of the Federal Building in downtown Chattanooga. He was a straight arrow, as far as I knew.

I nodded. "Yes, I know him," I said. "Was he one of Elizabeth's clients, too?"

She shook her head. "No, we didn't play that game," she said. "Liz's clients were hers, and mine were mine."

"Would you mind if we talk to him?" I asked.

She shrugged. "Sure. We have no secrets. I don't think he can help you, though. We were very discreet. I don't think he even knew Liz. But go ahead."

I nodded, then said, "So, you say you didn't think Archer killed her? Do you know who did?"

She raised her eyebrows. The blue eyes sparkled. She smiled and said, "Could have been any one of at least a dozen. Liz was a popular girl. She had some classy, powerful clients, including cops. People who didn't want their indiscretions made public and would do anything to make sure they weren't."

"Including your husband?" TJ asked.

"I told you; he wasn't one of her clients," she snapped.

"But she knew he was one of yours," TJ replied.

"She did, but Chester is one of those very few incorruptible officials that's immune to such things as blackmail, for instance. We've never made a secret of my past or our professional relationship. He had nothing to hide."

She grinned at TJ. "You're barking up the wrong tree, mister."

"So tell me," I said, changing the subject, "how did you and Elizabeth get your clients?"

She furrowed her brow and narrowed her eyes. "You don't know?" she asked.

"Err, no!" I said. "The escort industry is something I've never indulged in."

"Hah, get you," she said. "I, that is we, worked for… Lana Baudette. She advertised in the yellow pages. Can I ask you a question?"

"Of course," I replied.

"Why didn't you interview me?"

Yeah, why didn't I? I thought.

"Your name didn't come up," I replied. *Maybe it would have if I'd done my job*, I thought.

"D'you know how many clients Elizabeth had?" I asked.

She shook her head. "No, I don't, but it wasn't as many as you'd think. Liz was picky. Only the best for her. She wasn't taking new clients. Regulars? Twelve… fifteen. No more than that. As to names… she was also secretive. Charlie Stewart; I know she was seeing him. And there was a cop. She thought that was funny. He was a lieutenant, I think. She called him Tiny. There were others, too; cops, I mean. Higher-ups."

Finkle, I thought.

"Anyone else?" I asked.

She thought for a minute, then said, "Pitson. Greg Pitson. He had a couple of those payday loan shops. There was one on Rossville Boulevard and another in St. Elmo. She wasn't too keen on him, as I recall, but he could afford her, and he tipped well. There was a guy she called Mark. I don't know anything about him. And there was..."

She sucked on her bottom lip, put a hand to her mouth for a moment, then took it away and shook her head. "There was someone else. She talked to me about him several times, but I don't think she ever told me his name. I know she saw him regularly, and that he tipped well, which was why she kept seeing him. She didn't like him, though. She told me he liked it rough, and she wasn't into that. I think he frightened her. But... Well... She liked the money, I guess."

She paused and looked at the wedding ring on her left hand. "Look, there were more, but I don't know their names. You'll have to talk to Lana. You want to talk to Chester, go ahead, but it won't do you any good. He stuck to me like glue. That Christmas, he asked me to marry him, and I got out of that rat's nest. We've been together for over twenty years. You can't hurt either of us. I don't hide what I was. Neither does he. We're just about bulletproof. That's all I know."

"Thank you, Shirley," I said. "You've been most helpful." I stood up, handed her my card and said, "If you remember anything, anything at all, especially names, please call me. If there's ever anything I can do for you," I added and nodded at the card still in her hand, "call me."

She looked at the card, then at me and said, "I might just do that. It's nice to meet you both."

And with that, we left.

"So what d'you think?" TJ said as he pulled the car door shut.

"I believe her," I said. "And we have a couple of names to—"

"Yeah," TJ said, cutting me off. "And one of them was Henry Finkle. You caught that, right? Tiny?"

"I did," I said as I started the engine.

"You gotta let me do that one," he said. "I can't wait to tear the little shit from stem to stern."

"That's a bit drastic, don't you think?" I said, grinning.

"He's dirty," TJ growled. "And I don't like dirty cops. What now, Harry?"

"Back to the office, I think. I'm hoping Jacque has been able to make an appointment at Riverbend Max. I'd like to talk to Archer as soon as possible."

As it happened, Jacque had made an appointment for me. But I'm getting ahead of myself.

We grabbed a Subway sandwich and coffee on the way back and arrived at the office at just after two-thirty that afternoon.

"Jacque," I said as I walked through the outer office front door. "My office, and I want Tim and Heather there, too."

"Okay," I said when everyone was seated. "We have a lot to get through, so let's get on with it. First…" and then I filled them in on the details of our interviews with Joey Breen and Shirley Walker. Then I turned to Jacque and said, "How did it go with Riverbend?"

"You have an appointment at eleven-thirty tomorrow morning," she replied. "That, with the time change, gives you plenty of time to drive, if that's what you want to do."

I thought about it for a moment, then said, "I'll check with August, but yes, that's probably what I'll do. So, now we have that fixed, we can figure out what to do between now and Wednesday evening. We have names.

"Tim. I want you to do deep dives into the following: One, Captain Henry Finkle. I want to know everything there is to know. I want to know his financials, his social habits, his online activity, the works. I want to know when he takes a… Well, you get the idea. Two, Charles Stewart. He's an attorney, and he was one of Elizabeth Reynolds' clients. Three, Lana Baudette. She was a madam and Elizabeth's boss. Four, retired Sergeant Thomas "Tom" Miller. He was my boss. It was Tom who pushed for a quick solution. Five, Gregory Pitson. You'll love this one. He was, and I think he still is, a loan shark. He was also one of Elizabeth's clients. Got it?"

Tim stopped scribbling, looked up at me, nodded, and said, "Got it. When d'you need it."

"ASAP," I said.

"That's what I thought," he replied, dryly.

"Moving right along—" I began, but TJ cut me off.

"Hey. What about Chester Castle, Shirley's husband?" he asked

"We'll give him a pass for now," I said. "I believe what she had to say, and if what she says is true, they are both clean. So, moving right along," I said for the second time. "I'll interview David Archer tomorrow morning, and you, Heather, will talk to Charlie Stewart—"

"And I get Henry Finkle," TJ said, interrupting me with a huge grin.

"No!" I said. "You're coming to Nashville with me."

"Aww hell," he grumbled.

"Don't worry," I said. "We'll get to him; all in good time. Now, I have to talk to a man about a plane. I do not want to drive to Nashville unless I absolutely have to."

As it turned out, I didn't have to, thanks to my father, August.

10

I CLOSED THE MEETING AND CALLED MY FATHER. I CAUGHT HIM just as he was about to leave for the day.

My father is an attorney, a very good one. He's a high-end personal injury lawyer. I'm sure you've seen him on TV. His ads run on most local stations almost every day. What I'm trying to say without sounding like I'm bragging is that he's quite well off… No, that's an understatement; he's a billionaire. And, as most billionaires do, he owns a Gulfstream G280, which is why I made the call.

"Hey, Dad," I said when he answered my call. "Good day?"

"What d'you want, Harry?" He sounded tired.

"What, no hello?" I said.

"I've had a rough day, Harry," he replied. "I need some quiet time, and I need a drink. It's Monday afternoon. You never call on Monday afternoons. Ergo, you want something. So tell me what it is and let me go home in peace."

I smiled. "I'm interviewing a client in Nashville tomorrow morning and—"

"And you want to take the Gulfstream," he said, interrupting me.

"If it's convenient," I said. "You can bill me for the cost. You always do."

"Call Robert," he replied. "Tell him what you need. If it's convenient for him, yes…" He paused for a minute, then said, "Nashville?"

I grinned. I could almost see the frown.

"Yeah," I replied. "I'm going to interview David Archer at Riverbend."

He was silent for another moment, then said, "That's a hoary old chestnut. What's going on?"

"I thought you wanted to go home," I said.

"Oh, get on with it, Harry," he snapped. "What have you gotten yourself into this time?"

I sighed and gave him the short version, and when I'd finished, all he said was, "Extraordinary. Well, good luck. Keep me appraised. Call Robert." And he hung up.

Robert Maxwell was August's pilot. He and a crew of two—Jason Paxton, his copilot and Jane Samon, his flight attendant—were on call, but they usually needed at least a week's notice so, even though I had August's blessing, I still needed the crew to be free and available. As it happened, Robert and Jason were, but Jane was not, which meant we'd have to fend for ourselves, which was okay with me.

I told Robert to call when he'd filed his flight plan, and we agreed on wheels up at nine-thirty the following morning. Which meant, because of the time change, we'd be on the ground in Nashville around nine o'clock local time, which would give us time to eat breakfast before the interview.

I spent that Monday evening with Amanda, Jade, and Rose, August's second wife and my stepmother. She wanted to spend some time with Jade.

We put Jade to bed at eight and then the three of us sat together out on the patio beside the pool, chatting and watching the lights come on in the city below. It was a pleasant evening and, for the first time since Betty Markham showed up in my office, I was able to relax.

~

THE FOLLOWING MORNING, Tuesday, I arrived at the airport at eight-thirty to find TJ already there, waiting for me in the parking lot, and Robert was walking around the aircraft doing his pre-flight inspection. I've often wondered about that. Ostensibly, a pre-flight inspection of the exterior is to see if there's anything amiss, but how d'you do that? How would a pilot know? It's a puzzlement, don't you think?

We boarded the aircraft to find that Jason, the co-pilot, had coffee waiting. Not his job, but it was a nice thought.

What I like about flying private is that I didn't have to spend more time than I needed to in Nashville. I figured if all went well, I'd be back in my office by three that afternoon. That would not have been possible if I'd had to drive. Expensive? Of course. But my father was a billionaire, my company was successful, and my mother had left me… quite well off. So yes, I avoided a night-marish drive both ways. The traffic at both ends of the trip is always a problem, especially driving into Nashville.

The Riverbend Maximum Security Institution is located off Cockrill Bend Boulevard in Nashville, an easy twenty-minute drive from the airport on I-40. It's a forbidding-looking collection of two-story block-shaped buildings that house more than twenty-five-hundred male inmates. I've visited the prison more times than I want to remember, and I've always found it to be beyond depressing.

We took a taxi to the prison and arrived fifteen minutes before the appointed time. We navigated the security systems and were taken to a large public room wherein were maybe two-dozen tables with chairs, many of which were occupied by inmates and visiting family members. David Archer was not among them.

We were shown to a table, and we sat down together to wait. Five minutes later, David, accompanied by a guard, was escorted to our table.

"One hour," the guard said, then turned away and went to a seat under the window where he sat down to watch us.

"You look good," David," I said after he'd sat down opposite us.

"Screw you, Starke," he said, bitterly. "What d'you want?"

"I had a visit from your sister last Friday," I replied. "She said you had something to tell me."

He slowly shook his head, the corners of his mouth turned down in an ugly grimace.

When I told him he was looking good, I meant it. After more than twenty years behind bars, I'd expected him to look worn, even haggard, but he didn't. He was a big man, still only forty years old, but his hair had turned prematurely gray; his long face had a hollow look about it, but his eyes were bright and he looked fit, in good shape, and I assumed he worked out.

"What the hell she do that for?" he snarled. "I got nothin' to say to you."

"She thinks you're innocent," I said. "She asked me to help you."

"Hah!" he laughed, leaned back in his chair and folded his arms. "Why would she ask you, of all people? You're a cop. You put me in here."

"I'm not a cop anymore," I said. "I'm a private investigator, and this is TJ, my associate."

He stared at me. His forearms looked like a couple of hams. *Oh, yeah, he works out*, I thought.

"So?" he said, his eyes narrowed almost to slits.

I took Betty's letter from my inside pocket, laid it on the table, smoothed it out, then pushed it toward him.

The guard stood up. I put a hand up, looked at him, and nodded.

He nodded back, then slowly sat down again, watching Archer like a hawk.

Archer leaned forward, his arms still folded, looked at the letter, then leaned back in his chair again.

I looked at the guard as I retrieved the letter. He'd visibly relaxed.

I turned my attention back to Archer.

"So?" he repeated.

"You had an alibi," I said. "It could have proved your innocence. Why didn't you speak up?"

He shrugged. "I had my reasons."

"MaryAnn Williams," I said. It wasn't a question. It was a statement.

He nodded slightly but said nothing.

"You were there that night, weren't you?" I asked. "Two eyewitnesses put you there. You want to tell me about it?"

"What for?" he asked. "I already lost two appeals. There's nothin' you can do after all this time."

"Why don't you stop whining and talk to the man?" TJ said. "Stop feeling damn sorry for yourself and help us get you out of here."

"What the hell d'you know?" Archer snapped. "You have any idea what it's like in here? Hell can't be any worse than this."

"Yeah," TJ retorted. "As it happens, I do. I did three years for something I didn't do. Now stop whining and let's get on with it before they throw us out."

He glared at TJ but seemed to relax a little.

"Yeah, I was there," he began. "I was supposed to see MaryAnn at seven-thirty, but Liz called me. She had this client…

He scared the crap out of her. She'd seen him before, several times, so she said. She'd told me about him before. She said he liked it rough, that he liked to hurt her. She said the last time he'd grabbed her by the neck and choked her as he… finished. Know what I mean?"

I nodded, but didn't speak. I didn't want to interrupt his flow.

"She said he gave her the creeps. I remember laughing at her and asked how it was every client didn't give her the creeps."

He paused for a moment, a vacant look in his eyes, as if he was reliving the moment, then he continued, "Anyway," he said, "she told me she told him she couldn't see him that night. She made some excuse; I don't remember what it was, but he wasn't having it. Wouldn't take no for an answer, so she said. So she called me and asked me to come over, and I did. He was supposed to show up at eight, but he didn't. I waited till eight-thirty. I knew MaryAnn would be pissed, so I left. I called Liz at… it was just after nine to make sure she was okay. She was. She said he still hadn't turned up. I spent the next two hours with MaryAnn at the Island Motel out by the airport and then went home to find you waiting for me. I was with MaryAnn from about five minutes to nine until after eleven. She'll tell you."

"David," I said. "D'you know who the client was?"

Archer shook his head. "No," he replied. "I asked her, but she wouldn't tell me. All she'd say was that he was somethin' high up in the city. I don't know what she meant by that. Maybe it was him what killed her."

"And you're sure you don't know who he was?" I persisted. "You're not protecting—"

"I told yah, didn't I?" he snapped, cutting me off. "I don't know who he was. All right?"

I nodded. "I talked to Joey Breen," I said, changing the subject. "He said he heard you arguing with Elizabeth. What was that about?"

He made a face. "I was pissed," he said. "I had a date with MaryAnn and I was going to be late, and I knew she'd be pissed, too… And she was. Look, me and Liz were friends," he continued, "since we was kids. She was like a sister to me. We looked after each other, which is why I went there that night, but that doesn't mean I wanted to be there. So yes, we argued, but it was about nothin'."

"You weren't lovers?" TJ asked.

Archer looked at him as if he was some kind of lowlife and snarled, "Shit, no!"

"Why didn't you tell me all that?" I asked. "It would have made a difference."

"Yah think?" he snarled. "Shit! I couldn't talk to you. You were one of them. Not that I would have, anyway. Not with MaryAnn being married, an' all."

"One of them?" I asked, frowning. "What d'you mean?"

"You was a cop," he said. "They wanted a fall guy, and they wanted it quick so they could shove it all under the carpet. How many cops d'you think she was seeing? I can name two, but there were more. High-ups, too. Nah, I kept my mouth shut, and not just because I didn't want to get MaryAnn into trouble. I wanted to stay alive."

I looked at him in astonishment.

He leaned back in his chair, smiling. "Didn't know any of that, did yah?" he said.

"Who were they, David?" I asked, quietly.

He looked at me for a moment, as if considering what he was about to say. "Your boss, for one," he said. "Sergeant Miller. Now where d'you think he got the kind of money from to afford Liz? Not on a sergeant's pay, that's for damn sure. You know what she charged? Go on, guess."

I shook my head, stunned.

"Seven-fifty an hour," he said. "Seven-frickin'-fifty an hour," he repeated. "Can you believe that? How d'you figure Miller could afford that? He was a dirty cop, that's how, and so was his boss, that lieutenant… Fi…" He frowned, then said, "Finkle! That was his name. He was seeing her, too. And it was made pretty damn clear that I'd better keep my mouth shut, or else."

I shook my head. "How d'you know all that?" I asked, still not quite believing what I was hearing.

"She frickin' told me, is how," he replied. "And I seen 'em; both of 'em. I seen 'em there, at her apartment. They didn't see me, though. But I was watchin' out for her."

"You were her pimp?" TJ asked.

"Hell, no," he replied. "That was Lana; frickin' bitch."

"You said there were more cops," I said. "So, who else besides Miller and Finkle?"

"I don't know," he replied. "She said there were, but she didn't tell me their names, and I never saw 'em. I think they were outcalls, you know?"

I shook my head. If what he was telling me was the truth, we had a problem, a big problem. I was setting myself up to go against the Chattanooga Police Department, my onetime colleagues. And that was never good.

"What d'you know about an Amy Murphy?" I asked.

He frowned, then said, "Amy? Not much. I know she was an escort. Worked with Liz. They were good friends. She mentioned her now and then." He shrugged. "That's about it."

"Tell me about MaryAnn Williams," I said. "What part did she have to play in this mess?"

"Mess?" He scowled. "Frickin' mess? Are you kiddin' me? If it's a mess, it was your makin'. MaryAnn had nothin' to do with nothin'. You leave her be, got it?"

"Show some respect, you piece of shit," TJ snapped. "If it hadn't been for her, there would've been none of this. You wouldn't be here, and neither would we. Now answer the frickin' question."

Archer stared at him. There was no doubt he blamed me for where he was, but TJ was right. If MaryAnn had come forward in 2001, he probably wouldn't have been convicted.

"There's nothin' to tell," he said belligerently. "We… We were in love—still are. She was married to a piece of shit husband. We saw each other when we could; when she could get away. I told her to say nothin', that it would all work out. They'd find who killed her and… But you didn't look no further than me, did you, Starke?"

"So what's different now?" TJ said. "Why's she willing to give you an alibi now? And what makes you think anyone will believe it?"

He sighed and shook his head and, for the first time during the interview, he looked defeated.

"I told yah, she was married to a son of a bitch. I've not seen much of her over the past twen'y-one years. It's a long way for her to come. She got divorced. It came final three months ago. Since then, she's been here every week. We wanna get married. It's…" He trailed off, shaking his head. Then he looked at me and said, "I didn't do it, Starke. I don't know who did. But… if you can get me outta here…" He paused, then said. "There's no forgivin' you for what you didn't do back then, but… Ah, what the hell? What am I thinkin'?"

I looked at him for a moment, then said, "You're right, David. I can't give you back the years you've lost, but it wasn't my fault. You had an alibi. You chose not to provide it. That's on you. But what I can do is promise you that I'll do my damnedest to get you out of here."

He looked at me, pursed his lips and made a face. "So you say," he said, then turned and looked at the guard and nodded. "Say hello to Miller for me," he said, rising to his feet, "and to that piece o'shit Finkle."

I stared up at him. He nodded. The guard took his arm, turned him around, and escorted him out of the room.

"You believe him?" TJ said as we waited for the cab.

"I think I do," I said. "I didn't think much about it at the time, but now that I think about it, Miller was in one hell of a hurry to close the case. Finkle? Knowing how he treated Kate; yeah, I believe him. But higher-ups? I dunno, TJ. That may be a bit of a stretch. But we'll see, I guess. Let's hope MaryAnn will verify his alibi, and that she's believable."

11

It was three-forty-five when TJ and I walked into the outer office that afternoon. Jacque was standing beside Lucy at the front desk, watching her doing something on the computer.

She looked up as we entered and said, "Hey, you two. How did it go?"

I clamped my teeth together, made a face, then said, "Better than I expected. What's Tim doing?"

"What he's always doin'," she replied. "Skulking in that dungeon of his. Working on that list you gave him, I shouldn't wonder."

I nodded. "Give him a buzz," I said. "Ask him to join me in my office. You, too, Jacque, and Heather."

She nodded, leaned forward and said something to Lucy I didn't catch, then went to her office.

"You, too, TJ," I said, "but I need coffee first. How about you?"

He shook his head. "Not for me."

"My office, then," I said. "Five minutes."

I went to the break room, poured myself a large mug of coffee, added a splash of milk and then went up to my office.

Heather was the first to arrive, followed by Tim, Jacque, and finally TJ.

"So," I said. "Who wants to go first?"

"I will," Heather said. "I talked to Elizabeth Reynolds' friend Amy Murphy this morning." She looked at Tim.

Tim nodded and handed me a photo, a mug shot. "That's her," he said. "She has a rap sheet. She was arrested several times back in 1999, 2000 and 2001, for a variety of offences including solicitation and possession of drugs. There's nothing since May of 2001. Elizabeth Reynolds was murdered on July 12, 2001. Coincidence?"

"I doubt it," I said, looking at the photograph. "We don't believe in coincidences, do we?" I put the photo down and shook my head.

"Well, she knows you," Heather said, smiling. "Her exact words were, 'He's that crappy detective that put David in prison.'"

"Nice," I said, dryly. "What else did she have to say?"

"Not much," Heather replied. "She's working at a diner on Frazier. The diner was busy. She couldn't talk much. She told me she's no longer working as an escort, and that after David was arrested, she called in and left a request to speak with someone, but no one followed up on it."

"Really?" I said. "That doesn't sound right. Who'd she talk to? Does she remember?"

Heather shook her head, "Uh-uh! She doesn't remember, but she does remember the names of some of Elizabeth's clients. She also said Elizabeth had been her friend, that she, Elizabeth, had stood by her when she was strung out, which is why she called in. She's willing to talk to us, but not at the diner. I don't know if she's just paranoid, but she said she's certain she's being watched. She suggested The Sorbonne. I thought that was kinda creepy, but that's just me."

I thought about it for a moment, then nodded and said, "It's times like these I miss Benny. Sure, why not?"

"I'll set it up then," Heather said. "She gets off at five. What time would suit you?"

I shook off thoughts of Benny. "The Sorbonne opens its doors at four, so tonight. Say…" I looked at my watch. It was already after four. "No, tomorrow, at Six."

Heather nodded, then said, "Oh, and she told me to be sure to tell you that's she's been clean for fifteen years."

"Has she, now?" I said. "That's impressive. I wonder what happened."

"Tim," I said. "MaryAnn Williams?"

Tim looked up at me, seemingly startled. He put his hand to his mouth and coughed, then cleared his throat and said, "Yeah, her. Not much, I'm afraid. No record. Good credit. Reasonably well off. Married to Bob Williams for twenty-seven years. They divorced three months ago. No Facebook page. Not much of a digital footprint. Bob… Robert J. Williams, though, is quite another story. He's a successful banker—worth a pot full—and a long-time serving member of the city council. His name has also been mentioned as a potential US senatorial candidate. He's clean, as far as I can tell, but I can dig deeper if you want."

"Hold off on that for now," I replied. "Where does she live?"

He gave me an address off Gibson Pond Road.

"Good," I said. "Who else do we have?"

"Captain Finkle," he began, and TJ immediately perked up. "Charles Stewart, the customer, Lana Baudette, the madam, and your Sergeant Miller. Oh, and Gregory Pitson, your friendly neighborhood loan shark. Who d'you want first?"

"Finkle," TJ snapped.

I smirked and nodded.

"Captain Henry Finkle," Tim began. "Fifty-eight. Married to Lois Hazel Capper. Joined the force in 1988. Promoted quickly through the ranks to assistant chief. Demoted to captain in 2018 for sexual impropriety because of complaints by several unnamed female officers. In 2001, at the time of Elizabeth Reynolds' death, he was a detective lieutenant attached to the vice squad." He looked at me and asked, "Another coincidence?" I shrugged, and he continued. "Other than the impropriety demotion, he has a clean record. His credit is good, and… that's about it."

I looked at Jacque and said, "See if you can get me… No, I'll do it myself. Hold on."

I picked up my desk phone, put it on speaker, and punched in the number for the police department. It rang twice and a female voice answered, "Chattanooga Police Department. How can I help you?"

"Captain Finkle, please," I replied.

"Who's calling, please?" she asked.

"Harry Starke," I replied.

"Hold, please."

There was a moment of silence and then, "Harry Starke. What can I do for you?"

"I'd like to talk, Henry," I said. "When can I drop by?"

He was quiet for a moment, then said, "What d'you want to talk about?"

"Elizabeth Reynolds," I said. "Remember her?"

The silence was longer this time, then he said, "I don't… I'm not… That's old news, Harry. It was your case. What's to talk about?"

"I'm not sure," I said, "which is why I want to talk to you."

I could almost see him shaking his head. "As I said, it was your case. I had nothing to do with it. So no, I don't think so."

"Hmm," I said, "that's a shame, Henry. You see, I don't think Archer killed her. And if that's true, then somebody else did. Tom was pushing me to close it out quickly and according to him, it was you that was applying the pressure. Henry, I'm going to bust this thing wide open. So, now would be a good time for you to talk to me."

Again, there was a lengthy silence until, "Very well, but not here. The Boathouse at one tomorrow." And he hung up.

I looked at TJ and nodded. "You want in?" I asked.

"You'd better believe it," he growled.

"Good," I said. "We'll go see MaryAnn tomorrow morning and then Henry at one."

"I can't wait," he said, and I turned again to Heather.

"Heather," I said. "You and I will keep the appointment with Amy Murphy at six tomorrow. You good with that?"

She nodded, and I turned again to Tim. "Tell me about the shark," I said.

He shoved his glasses further up the bridge of his nose, flipped through several screens on his iPad, then looked at me and said, "He's a nasty one, is Gregory Pitson. He took over the business from his father, Frank Pitson, when he died in a hit and run in January 1993. Frank was a bad one, but he has nothing on Greg. He is, as we know, a loan shark, but strangely, he doesn't have a rap sheet, not one that I can find, anyway. He's known for brutality. You don't pay, he hurts you. Well, not him. He has a pair of nasties that do the hurting for him. He still has the two payday loan shops, but they appear to be fronts for his other nefarious financial activities. And, as we know from your interview with Shirley, he was also one of Elizabeth's regular clients. You want more?"

"No," I replied, "that's enough for now. "Kate and I will interview him Thursday morning."

I thought for a moment, then nodded. She was indeed capable. "Okay, that leaves the attorney Charles Stewart. He was also one of Elizabeth Reynolds' clients. My old boss, Tom Miller and Lana Baudette. She was Elizabeth's boss. So, Tim?" I asked.

He nodded, did his thing with his glasses, scrolled some more, and then said, "Lana Baudette. Fifty-two. Onetime model turned escort turned madam. French immigrant parents. Both are still alive. Surprisingly clean record. Small digital footprint. Exclusive address. No registered phone number. No personal social media. Arrested once for prostitution, but the charges were dropped for lack of evidence. Finances? All aboveboard: taxes filed and paid promptly. Known associates: Charles Stewart, attorney; Walter Keighley, councilman-at-large, and…" He looked up at me, then continued in a low voice, "Gordon Whacker—"

"Assistant police chief Gordon Whacker?" I said, interrupting him. "Well, well. What about that? I want—"

"Already done, boss," Tim said. "He's clean, and I mean squeaky; totally."

I nodded. "I don't believe it. Keep digging. And check out this Walter Keighley. If he's a known associate of Lana, there has to be something; same for Stewart. What d'you have on him? And don't call me boss. What else?"

Tim grinned and shook his head. "Yes, sir." He frowned, then said, "Charles Stewart is a prominent defense attorney. He seems to be on the up-and-up. No complaints. Excellent record. Maybe your dad…"

"Yeah, maybe," I said. "I'll give him a call. Right now, that leaves Miller. What do we know about him?"

"He retired as a lieutenant four years ago, in 2018, with an exemplary record. Nothing there, either."

"Geez," I muttered. "There has to be something. The more I think about it, the more I'm convinced he had an agenda." I heaved a deep breath, then said, "Oh well, we'll figure it out, I'm sure." I looked at my watch. It was just after five.

"I'm bushed," I said. "Let's call it a day. We'll meet here at eight-thirty tomorrow morning and finalize things. Any questions?"

There were none, so I wrapped it up and we all went home; me with my head in a whirl.

It had been one hell of a day, and I had a gut feeling it was going to be another tomorrow.

And, these days, I always trust my gut.

12

FOR THE FIRST TIME IN A WEEK, I SLEPT WELL THAT NIGHT. I ROSE early the following morning and went for a run.

It was still dark. The moonless, cloudless sky was a field of brilliant stars. The air, ten degrees lower on the mountain than in the city below, was crisp and refreshing as I pounded the deserted streets, the anomalies of the Reynolds case forefront in my mind.

Why didn't MaryAnn come forward, regardless of Archer's wishes? I wondered. *She let him fester in prison for twenty-one years. It makes no sense. Anyone who purports to be as fond of someone as she does would have said to hell with it and done her best to set him free. Maybe we'll find out today.*

I turned west onto Scenic Highway and then north onto West Brow and headed home. It wasn't my usual six miles, but I ran at a good clip and burned the necessary calories.

And what about Archer? I wondered, still not sure how much of his story I believed. I shook my head. *What the hell was I doing back then? There was so much more I could have, and should have, done. Why did I not know about Amy Murphy? Or Shirley Walker? Geez, what a screwup. I can't wait to talk to Finkle... and Tom. And what about him? It had to be some kind of cover-up, and he had to have been right in the middle of it. Son of a bitch! But if Archer didn't kill her, and I'm pretty damn sure he didn't, then who did?*

And what do I really know about the victim? Not one whole hell of a lot! I sure as hell did a lousy job of an investigation. I took everything at face value. Archer looked good for it. He was at the scene. He was heard arguing with her. He had no alibi. It was enough to convict, and he was. But now? Whew! I shook my head as I turned into my drive, stopped, stretched, my hands on my hips, breathing hard.

Well, let's see what today brings, was my final thought before heading into the house.

It was a little after six-forty-five when I walked into the kitchen, showered, dressed and ready to face whatever the day might throw at me.

Amanda had coffee waiting. "Pleasant run?" she asked as she poured me a cup. "You want breakfast?"

I shook my head. "No, I'll get something later, and yes, it was," I replied. "It's gorgeous out there. It's going to be another beautiful day… but I have an appointment at six this evening, at the Sorbonne, of all places, so I'll be late home. Does that mess with your plans?"

She shook her head. "No. I'll drop Jade off at school, then go into work until three. I'm going to record a segment for the six o'clock news and then I'll be done."

I grinned at her over my cup and said, "How can it be news if it's pre-recorded?"

She smiled at me and made a face. "That's the magic of television," she replied. "What about you? Busy day?"

"An interesting day," I replied. "I'm interviewing Archer's alibi; I hope. And then I have an interview with that louse Henry Finkle. That should be interesting. Maybe even fun. TJ's champing at the bit."

"TJ, huh? Isn't it about time he retired?" she asked.

"Oh, my Lord," I said. "Never let him hear you say that. He'll have a conniption."

"How old is he now?" she asked.

"Seventy-three, but you'd never know it. He's in better shape than I am. No joke!"

She shook her head. "He has a… a certain reputation," she said.

"You mean he's tough?" I said. "Hell, yes, he's tough. He saved my life twice. He can do no wrong as far as I'm concerned."

She nodded. "Just be careful, Harry," she said. "There are a lot of people out there who would be happy to see you brought down. Shady almost managed it. So did Calaway."

"But he didn't, and she didn't, thanks to you," I replied. "You worry too much, Amanda. I'm surrounded by good people. Okay, enough chat," I said, standing up. "I need to go. See you tonight. Kiss Jade for me."

I gave my wife a quick kiss, slipped my compact CZ Shadow into its holster and left her to sort out Jade and Maria, who walked in as I walked out.

It was twenty minutes after eight when I walked into my reception area. Lucy was already at her desk. Jacque was out back in the break room, Tim in his lair, Heather in her office and TJ in his. I grabbed a cup of coffee, asked Jacque to gather everyone in the conference room, and then I went and sat down to wait. By eight-thirty, everyone was present.

"All right, everyone," I said. "I need something to eat, so this won't take long." And I went over the details of what we'd discussed the previous evening, finishing by saying, "Heather, I want you to poke around, talk to your CIs, then you and I are meeting Amy at six. You good with that?"

She nodded.

"TJ, you and I are set until after we're done with Henry. That leaves Miller, Baudette and Stewart. We'll talk about them later, but we need to get them interviewed tomorrow, if everything goes as planned today, that is. We're all good then?"

They all nodded and began rising to their feet.

"Then let's do it," I said.

~

IT WAS a thirty-minute drive to MaryAnn Williams' address off Gibson Pond Road. So, after a quick stopover at Hardee's for a sausage and egg biscuit, we arrived outside the rather expansive one and a half story home at a little after nine-forty-five. I parked the car on the road in front of the house and together, TJ and I walked the short drive to the three steps that led up to the front porch.

"Nice place," TJ said appreciatively. "These folks have some money."

"I think it's the husband who has the money," I said. "She must have gotten the house in the divorce settlement."

I pressed the button on the video doorbell, and we waited.

Less than a minute later, the door opened and… The woman's looks belied her age. I knew she'd turned fifty, but she didn't look a day over thirty-five, though there were subtle signs of the plastic surgeon's work: her neck was a little too tight and her lips a little too full. The overall result, though, was to be applauded. She was, and always had been, an attractive and wealthy woman, which made me wonder, *What the hell does she see in Archer, an auto mechanic with little going for him other than his looks? Maybe it's a Lady Chatterley's Lover kind of thing. And why she would choose to be with a man who's serving a life sentence is beyond me.*

All that went through my mind before she could say, "You're Mr. Starke, aren't you?"

"MaryAnn Williams?" I asked. I didn't recognize her, but she obviously knew who I was.

She nodded and said, "I've been expecting you. Please, come in." And she stepped aside for us to enter.

She led us through the house to the kitchen, where she invited us to sit down at the extensive, granite-covered island.

"Can I get you some coffee?" she asked.

We both said no thank you.

"Well, I'm going to have some," she said, smiling. And she turned to one of the countertops and poured coffee into a bone china cup.

While she was doing it, I took a moment to appraise her and her surroundings.

Her highlighted hair was styled in much the same way as Amanda's. She calls it a pixie cut, but what do I know? Her makeup was subtle and carefully applied, exentuating the high cheekbones and full lips. She was a class act, and again I had to wonder what this obviously sophisticated woman saw in Archer.

At the center of the island were two silver-framed photographs. One of a young man and woman whom I assumed was her son and daughter, and the other—I picked it up and looked at it—was of a young couple I recognized as MaryAnn and David Archer.

Having poured the coffee, she set the cup and saucer down at the end of the island, then leaned forward, took the photograph from me, and set it down again.

"That was taken a month before he was charged," she said. "Now, please, proceed."

"This is my associate, TJ Bron," I said as she picked up her cup. "You obviously know who I am and why I'm here, so I'll get right to the point. It's possible you could have kept David out of prison. Why didn't you?"

"You really are forthright, aren't you, Mr. Starke?" she replied, smiling. "Yes, you're right. It's entirely possible I could have, but it was complicated… David insisted he wouldn't be convicted and that I must not ruin my marriage, not that there was much left of it to ruin, but I had two young children to consider. He himself was the product of a broken home, and he didn't want my children to suffer as he had. I know what you're thinking, Mr. Starke, but I loved him then and I still do. I…" She closed her eyes for a brief moment, then opened them and said, "I loved my children more. I hate myself for what I've done. There's not a day goes by that I don't regret it. But it is what it is, and now, now that I'm divorced, if I can, I want to put it right."

Well, I thought. *What can I say to that?*

I just nodded and said, "Why now? Why the divorce after all these years?"

She looked at me as if I was crazy, then her expression softened, and she said, "Time and place, Mr. Starke. Time and place. My husband, Tom, is a son of a bitch, if you'll pardon my language. He is, to quote the Bible, all things to all people, but, unlike Paul, that doesn't mean he saves some of them. No, Bob is all about Bob. He is a deviant, though you wouldn't know it. He covers it well. He's had more affairs that I can count. There's always someone somewhere. And he likes his sex…" She trailed off, looked at her fingernails, then said without looking up, "I don't want to talk about it."

"It's okay," I said, "I get the picture."

I looked at TJ and nodded.

"Where was your husband that night?" TJ asked, gently.

She looked up at him, frowning. "He was… home, all night. Why d'you ask?"

"Just procedure," TJ said. "But you were out, were you not?"

I could see where he was going with it.

She nodded, then said, "Yes, from seven-fifteen until eleven… ish. Bob was home. And he was…" Again, she trailed off. "… upset doesn't describe it. But I was with David from a few minutes before nine until fifteen minutes to eleven. I know that because I checked my watch. I had to be home by eleven, you see?"

"So you don't know if your husband was home all night or not?" TJ insisted.

She looked at him wide-eyed, and I could tell it wasn't something she'd ever thought of.

"But he had to be," she said. "The children… Oh, my God. He must have left them alone. They were just babies. You don't think—"

"We don't think anything," I said, quickly cutting her off. "We're just re-investigating the facts."

She bit her lip and stared down at the granite worktop. I looked at TJ. He smiled at me. I got the message. Someone was going to have to talk to Bob Williams.

She took a deep breath and said. "I was with David. He didn't kill that whore. I can prove it."

She reached under the counter and brought up a small wooden box. She opened it and took out four Polaroid photos of her and David Archer. They were, to say the least, risqué, and they were dated, on the back, in black ink.

I took them from her, looked at them, glanced at TJ, then handed them to him. He looked at them and handed them back to me.

I, in turn, handed them back to MaryAnn and said, "Unfortunately, Mrs. Williams, they don't help. They could have been taken anytime. But I get it. I don't think you're lying, so they help me. I don't think David killed her. I think she was his friend, and she was in trouble, and he tried to help. It was unfortunate he didn't wait a little longer. But, as you say, it is what it is. The alibi you provide, in and of itself, is also not enough. A lawyer, even a bad one, would argue that we have only your word. Three appeal judges wouldn't buy it. We need more. We need to find the real killer." Geez, I must sound like that guy on *Cold Case Files*.

"Can you do that?" she asked. "Really? Can you?"

"I, that is we, will do our best," I said. "Unfortunately, a lot of time has passed and, well, we'll do our best. I promise."

It was weak. I knew it, and I knew she knew it. But she nodded and thanked us both, and we left her standing at the front door, her eyes wet, biting her bottom lip.

13

WE NEED TO TALK TO WILLIAMS," TJ SAID AS WE WALKED BACK to the car.

"Indeed, we do," I agreed, "and we will. We'll add him to the list. Did he know Elizabeth? Did he take advantage of her services? Was he the client she was waiting for that night? She all but said he likes it rough. Interesting, don't you think?" I said, as I pulled the car door shut.

"Just another pervert," TJ said, stoically, as he pulled the seat-belt across his chest. "He likes to hurt people: so do I. I want to be there when you talk to him. And here's another thought for you, Harry. She's Archer's alibi, right? What if he's hers? What if he's been covering for her all these years?"

I glanced sideways at him, stared at him for a moment, then started the car and said, "Geez, TJ. Where the hell did that come from? That's warped."

"Nope," he replied as I made a U-turn and headed back into the city. "It's pragmatic."

"It would be one hell of a stretch," I said, "though it would explain why she never came forward, despite Archer forbidding her to do so. If she loves him as she said she does, it's hard to believe she'd let him rot in prison all these years."

"Yeah, that, too," TJ said. "Here's another thought for you: did they do a rape kit on the victim? And if they did, does the PD still have it?"

I nodded. "We did, but the results were inconclusive. Does the PD still have it?" I said. "I'm sure they do… they should. I'll ask Kate to look into it."

"Maybe they should send it for retesting," TJ said. "Maybe the new technology will reveal something. Or maybe someone was paid off, and the results were doctored."

I called Kate.

"Hey, Harry," she said. "What's up?"

"I'm not sure," I replied. "It's the Archer case. They did a rape kit on the victim. It should still be in the evidence box. I'd like to have it retested."

"And you want me to get it for you?" she asked dryly.

"Yes, please," I replied. "But you'd better run it by Johnston first. Though I can't see him having a problem with it."

"I'll see what I can do," she replied. "That it?"

"One more thing," I said. "It's been bugging me for years. There was a ring, a Tiffany engagement ring. It was found at the scene. I'd like to take another look at it."

"Got it," she said. "Anything else?"

"You're busy," I said.

"Aren't I always?"

"Thanks, Kate," I said, and hung up.

"We've got an hour or so before we meet with Finkle," I said. "Heather should be talking to Stewart. How about we go talk to my old boss, Tom Miller?"

I glanced at him. He was grinning like a barracuda in the middle of a school of herring.

"I can go for that," he said.

THE ADDRESS I had for Miller was on Tricia Drive, which is off Jersey Pike about fifteen minutes from the Boathouse, so I figured we had about an hour to spare before my appointment with Captain Henry Finkle. He didn't know I was taking TJ with me. I figured it would be a pleasant surprise for him, or not.

Miller's was an older home, modest, built sometime in the seventies. Set back from the road some fifty feet or so, the rancher was fronted by an expanse of lawn, close cropped but badly in need of water.

I parked on the drive and we walked to the front step and rang the bell. There was an immediate yapping on the other side of the door, which was quickly opened to reveal a much older version of the Tom Miller I once knew.

He'd been retired since 2012 and looked every day of his seventy-five years. He seemed to have shrunk. His back was bent, his head was bald, his chin covered in gray stubble, and he had a small, tan Chihuahua-mix in his arms.

"Harry?" he said, frowning, surprise written all over his face.

"Hello, Tom," I said. "Mind if we come in?"

"What d'you want?" he asked, but didn't move.

"Just to talk," I replied.

"What about?" he asked.

"Oh, come on, Tom," I said. "You going to make us stand out here on the step? I just want to chat about old times, is all."

The frown intensified. "Old times? What're you talkin' about, Harry?"

I locked eyes with him. He held it for a moment, then seemed to crumple. His shoulders slumped. He closed his eyes, then opened them again, stepped back and held the door open while cradling the dog in his other arm.

"You'll have to 'scuse the mess," he said. "I live alone, and the cleaning lady doesn't come until tomorrow. Sit yourselves down." He waved a hand at the aging couch covered in newspapers. "You want something to drink, or something?"

"I'm good," I said. "This is TJ Bron, my associate."

"Associate, huh?" he said, dropping into the worn recliner opposite the couch. "I heard you were doing good. You look good, too. The PI business must be suiting you."

"It's not so bad," I replied. "How about you, Tom?"

"Eh, one day after another," he replied. "Jess died two years ago. Breast cancer. The kids don't give a shit. Drop by once, maybe twice a month to see if I'm still breathin'. That's about it. I ain't hurtin' for money, though. Social security and my LT's pension provide the necessities, but little else. But you ain't here to enquire about my well-being. So what is it you want?"

I stared at him for a moment then plunged right it. "I'm re-investigating the Elizabeth Reynolds case," I said, watching him. Other than a slight smile, he didn't react.

"So," he said, "that's it, huh? That was your case, Harry. You closed that one, and pretty damn quick, as I recall."

"On your insistence, as I recall," I replied, mimicking him.

"Don't you lay that one on me, Harry. You were the lead. It was your call."

"True," I said, "but, as I remember it, you were the one who applied the pressure. It was you who insisted we needed a quick result. You told me that twice during that first forty-eight. You told me someone was putting pressure on Finkle. You remember that, Tom?"

He looked away, down, and to the left. Inwardly, I shook my head. *You know better than that, Tom*, I thought.

"I never said that," he muttered.

"Yeah, you did," I said. "That, and more. Who was it, Tom? Who was putting pressure on Finkle? Was it Whacker?"

He looked startled. "I don't know what you're talkin' about," he said. "As to what I know, there was plenty of evidence it was Archer that killed her. Enough to put him away, and we did. It was a good result."

"What if it wasn't?" I said. "What if he's innocent? What if he has an alibi for that night?"

He stared at me; his eyes wide. "You're shitting me," he said.

"Not hardly," I replied. "He has an alibi. He didn't do it. Now spill it. Who wanted the case closed? Was it Whacker?" I asked again.

"I don't know..." he trailed off, then said, "You need to go. I've said all I'm going to. Now get the hell out of here."

"Were you dirty, Miller?" TJ asked, quietly.

Even I was shocked by the out-of-the-blue question. Miller looked stunned.

"Wh...at? What the hell is that?" he bellowed. "I never took a dirty dime in my life."

"But you did give in to pressure from above, didn't you?" TJ insisted.

Miller's face was red with anger. He was spluttering with rage. Even the dog, still in his arms, looked upset.

"Screw you, you son of a bitch," he snarled. "I served thirty-five years without a blemish. I have five commendations. I—"

"But you did give in to pressure from above, didn't you?" TJ repeated the question, smiling.

"I... I..." He couldn't get the words out.

"Didn't you?" TJ insisted, still smiling.

Miller lay back in his chair, his head tilted back on the head-rest, his eyes closed. And he stayed like that for more than a minute. TJ and I said nothing.

And then, without moving or opening his eyes, he said, "It was Henry. He wanted it closed. I don't know why. He never said. Only that he was taking heat from someone, but he never said who. That's it. That's all I know."

"Tom," I said. "I didn't get a lot of help from you or anyone else, and I have to wonder why. What I do know is that there were cops who were clients of Reynolds. You were one. Henry was another. Who else was there?"

He looked at me as if I'd shot him.

"Me?" he said. "I…"

"Don't bother to deny it." I said. "It came from a good source. She was expensive, Tom. How were you able to afford it?"

His face was white. He was visibly stressed, breathing heavily. Then he seemed to calm down a little.

"It was just… a few times," he said. "She… And… Well… I looked the other way. Made sure she wasn't bothered. You know how it is. Quid pro quo. No harm done, right?"

"So you took bribes?" TJ said, caustically.

"It wasn't like a bribe," he replied. "It was like one favor for another."

"Where were you that night between nine and eleven?" TJ asked.

"Aee hell," he snapped. "You can't be serious. You think I… You're out of your frickin' mind. I don't know where I was. I wasn't with Liz, that's for damn sure."

"All right," I said. "That's enough of that. Tell me about Whacker. He's a known associate of Lana Baudette, Reynold's madam, pimp, or whatever you want to call her."

Miller shook his head. "That's news to me," he replied. "He was an assistant chief until he retired… four years ago, I think. I never had much to do with him, as you probably know, Harry."

I did know. I also knew Whacker, slightly. He was a shadowy

figure, always dressed in jeans and casual shirts. If you didn't know who and what he was, you'd never guess.

"And Henry?" I asked. "I know he was a client. Was he doing favors, too?"

He shrugged. "Your guess is as good as mine," he said. "Look, Harry. That's it. I swear. She was a nice girl. She was also so damn hot. I just..." Again, he shrugged. "I'm only human. It was on the table. I took it."

I stood up. Looked down at him and said, "You know, Tom, for some reason I can't explain, I believe you. We're going to leave now. It might be best if you kept our visit to yourself. You never know who you might piss off."

"And you?" he said. "You'll say nothing?"

"Keep the faith, Tom," I said. "Keep the faith. Don't get up. We'll see ourselves out."

And with that, we left. I stopped at the door, looked back at him and nodded. He just stared back at me. And I stepped through the door and pulled it closed behind me.

"You said you believed him," TJ said as we walked back to the car. "Did you?"

"Strangely enough, I did," I replied. "What he did was not unusual. Temptation is always there in one form or another. Some fall for it. Most don't. Tom, I think, was one of the few that did."

"That, in my mind, makes him a dirty cop," TJ said as he pulled the car door closed.

"Of course," I agreed and started the engine. "And there's no excuse for it. Was he a good cop? Aside from that indiscretion, yes, I think so. As he said, he has five commendations, so he must have done something good."

"Fifty shades of bullshit," TJ muttered. "I'm surprised at you, Harry."

"Yeah well," I said. "Me, too, sometimes, but I get over it."

"How about you, Harry? Did you ever bend the rules?" he asked.

I glanced sideways at him and said, "Never!"

"There you go then," he said. "Case closed."

I grinned at him as I turned onto Bonny Oaks and headed west toward Riverside Drive, the Boathouse Rotisserie & Raw Bar, and our date with destiny, or should I say Captain Henry Finkle.

14

Captain Henry Finkle! A name to be feared, at least by some. Known around the PD as Tiny, because of his diminutive stature, but not to his face, he was just five-eight, slim, maybe a hundred and forty pounds, age unknown, at least to the general populace of the department. I figured him to be in his mid-fifties, but appearances are deceptive, and he could have been older, though his brown hair had yet to show the first gray hair. His thin face, high cheekbones, thin nose, and beady black eyes and overall demeanor reminded me of a hungry rat. He was a bigot, a misogynist and a sexual predator, to which Kate can attest. Twice she reported him for harassment; the second time resulted in his demotion from assistant chief to captain and his reassignment from Homicide to Vice, something he's never forgiven her for, but was quite relevant to the Archer case; not then, but in 2022, when this story takes place.

We were to meet him at one o'clock. He was, of course, fashionably late, arriving at fifteen after. Not that it mattered. It was a beautiful day, and TJ and I were at a table overlooking the river.

"Harry," he said, full of bluster, his hand outstretched as far as it would go as he hurried toward us. "Sorry I'm late. Hope you haven't been waiting long. Pressures of work, you understand."

"Just enjoying the day," I said as I stood up and shook his hand. TJ stayed put, lounging eloquently in his seat. "You know TJ, of course," I said as I sat down again.

"TJ," he said. "Nice to see you."

I could see by the frown on his face that it wasn't, but he took a seat with his back to the river.

"Drink?" I asked. "We haven't ordered yet."

He looked at the bottle next to my glass and said, "Blue Moon? I see you haven't changed since you left the force. I'll have the same."

I caught the waiter's eye and ordered three more drinks: two Blue Moon and a Modelo for TJ.

"So! The Reynolds case," he said. "You're re-investigating it? May I ask why?"

"Simple," I replied. "Archer didn't do it."

"Hmm," he said. "If that's true, it doesn't look good for you, Harry. You put him away. What's it been? Twenty… twenty-one years?"

"Twenty-one," I said. "And it's true. He has an alibi."

Finkle's eyebrows raised. "After all this time?" he asked. "Really?"

"Really," I replied, "and that begs the question, who did kill Elizabeth Reynolds?"

He shook his head. "Really, Harry, I would have thought you'd have known better by now. Alibis are always suspect, especially when they spring up out of nowhere. Who is the obliging female? It was a female, wasn't it?" He smiled that insipid smile he was so famous for. I opened my mouth to reply, but TJ beat me to it.

"It makes no never mind who it was," he growled. "We

believe her, and that's all it takes for us to do a little digging. You were one of Reynolds' clients. Why don't you tell us about that?"

He sat bolt upright, put his hands on the arms of his chair and began to rise, saying, "I—"

But before he could complete the thought, TJ snapped out, "Sit down, Henry. Before I make you. And listen up. We know, okay. You want it broadcast around the PD, or d'you want it kept on the QT?"

Slowly, he lowered himself back onto his seat. The look on his face was priceless: a cross between a frown and a sneer. It made him look more like a rat than ever.

"You better have something to back that allegation up," he snarled.

"Let's just say it came from an impeccable source." TJ grinned at him, then added, "Two impeccable sources."

"What sources?" he asked.

"Really, Henry," he said, "I would have thought you'd have known better by now.".

"Touché!" he said without humor.

"We also know you're an associate of Lana Baudette, Reynolds' pimp," TJ said. "Comments?"

Me? I couldn't help but grin to myself as Finkle struggled to find something to say.

"Bullshit," he said, finally. "Whoever told you that is lying. I don't know this Baudette woman, and I certainly had nothing to do with the Reynolds girl."

"Really?" TJ said, lightly. "Hmm, now that's a little awkward." He looked at me, his eyebrows raised. I shrugged, so he leaned forward and continued, "Let's say that's true, Henry. And let's say a good friend of ours decided she didn't believe you and decided to open her own investigation. How d'you think that would go down?"

Henry stared at TJ, his face white, his left foot tapping on the floor.

It was at that moment the waiter arrived with our drinks. We waited until he left, then TJ said, "Well?"

"Gazzara?" he muttered, looking at me. "You wouldn't."

I gifted him with a huge smile and slowly nodded my head.

"Henry," I said, quietly. "There's no getting around it. What TJ said is easily confirmed. You were a client and because you were, Baudette has you in her pocket. There was a major cover up. You pressured Tom Miller, and he pressured me, but we know there was someone in a high place pressuring you. We think it was Gordon Whacker. Now, you want to talk to us or to Internal Affairs?"

He was quiet for a long moment, then said, "It was not what you think—"

"It never is," TJ said, dryly, interrupting him.

I gave TJ a warning look, then said, "Carry on, Henry."

"It wasn't what you think," he repeated. "I… I—"

"You were screwing her," TJ interrupted him again.

Finkle shrugged, sucked in his top lip as he stared down at the tabletop. "Okay," he said. "I—"

"Are you ready to order?" our waiter said, smiling down at us.

I leaned back in my seat, frustrated beyond description, heaved a sigh, looked up at him and said, "Give us a few minutes. I'll let you know when."

He nodded, a little put out, I thought, and left.

"Henry?" I said.

"It's true, I was seeing her," he said. "And no, there was no extortion. I was paying her the going rate. Not often. Every six or seven weeks. I'm not proud of it, but that's all it was."

"You were paying her seven-fifty a pop?" TJ asked. "I don't believe it. Where'd you get that kind of money?"

"Seven-fifty?" he asked, incredulously. "Where d'you get that? I paid her two-fifty. And she was worth every dime."

TJ looked at me. I shrugged slightly. "Go on, Henry," I said.

"That's it," he said. "That's all there was. I told you it wasn't what you were thinking."

"But you were pressuring Miller to get me to close it quickly," I said.

"Damn right I was," he replied. "I didn't want it to get out; what I was doing."

"Was someone pressuring you, Henry?" I asked. "Whacker, perhaps?"

"Whacker?" he asked, frowning evasively. He thought for a minute, then shrugged and said, "Well, he did mention it would be a good thing if we could close the case quickly…" He trailed off, staring at me, then said, "You don't think—"

"I don't think anything, Henry," I said. "I go by the facts."

"I just thought he was screwing her, too," he said. "I mean, I wasn't the only one. There were others."

"Such as?" I asked.

"I don't know," he replied, squinting at me. "And I didn't want to know. That kind of knowledge can get you into trouble. Me? Yeah, but that's all it was. I liked the girl, and yeah, I was pissed when she died, and I wanted you to get the killer. We all thought it was Archer, even you. Now. I'm done! I'm saying no more." And with that, he stood up.

"Was someone paying you off, Henry?" I asked, looking up at him.

He stared down at me. "Not only no, but hell no!" And then he turned away and stalked off through the restaurant, past the goggling waiter and out the front door.

"Well," TJ said, "that went well."

I nodded, deep in thought.

"So, what d'you think?" he asked.

"I think he was telling the truth," I said. "Where's that waiter?"

15

I DROPPED TJ OFF AT THE OFFICE WITH INSTRUCTIONS TO WRITE UP his thoughts of the day's events, then I spent a few minutes with Jacque in my office before I was to meet with Heather.

I made a few calls, checked the Reynolds file one last time, then told Jacque I'd see her the following morning and left for the Sorbonne, something I hadn't done since my friend Benny Hinkle was murdered there.

Heather was already there, seated in a booth, drink in hand. She waved, and I joined her. It was ten minutes to six.

We talked about our day, the case, and our thoughts; none of it was very productive. But that's what you get when you're making small talk to pass the time. Six o'clock rolled by, then fifteen after, then six-thirty, and by then I was beginning to think something was wrong. By seven, I was sure of it.

"I think we should go check out the restaurant where she works," Heather said.

I agreed, paid the check, and then followed her as she drove across town to the Electric Diner.

We parked side-by-side and went inside. The place was all but deserted. Heather stepped up to the counter, spoke to one of the women, and asked for the manager.

"She was fine when she left at the end of her shift," she stated.

"When was that?" Heather asked.

"Five-thirty," she replied. "She was in a bit of a hurry. She said she had an appointment."

Heather turned, looked meaningfully at me, and said, "We have to assume that was her appointment with us. I don't like it, Harry."

Neither did I, but I didn't say so. Instead, I suggested we trace the route we thought she would have taken to the Sorbonne, which is what we did. We took my car and drove slowly back across town.

There were a couple of routes she could have taken. We chose the most direct one and… Nothing, so we went back to the diner and took the more circuitous route. Again, nothing.

We gave it up, and I was driving Heather back to the diner via the direct route to get her car when she spotted something.

"Hey," she said. "Slow down. Look over there. That car."

I slowed and, on a cleared lot, I could see a car, a pale blue, 2017 model Toyota Corolla. It wouldn't have been so noticeable had not the driver's side door been wide open. I made a U-turn and drove back to the lot, parked on the road, and we stepped out onto the asphalt.

We walked around the Corolla, peering inside. There was a Styrofoam cup with a straw in the cupholder, some nondescript bric-a-brac on the back seat, but little else.

I took out my phone and called Kate, hoping she was still at work; she wasn't, but she took my call. I explained where I was and why I'd called her and then asked her if she could have someone run the Corolla's plate. She took the number and said she'd call me back and, five minutes later, she did. The car was registered to Amy Murphy. Kate said she'd be there in twenty minutes, and I was not to touch anything. As if!

As promised, she arrived some twenty minutes later in a flurry of action, followed by a blue and white cruiser and a CSI tow truck.

"Boy, you don't let up, do you?" she said. "Right after you called, I received another call from Traffic. They found a body five miles away in an alley off Minton Street, an area notorious for drug trafficking. And I'm betting it's your Amy Murphy."

I looked at Heather. She nodded. "You want us to take a look?" I asked. "Heather knows Amy. If it is her, she'll know."

Kate nodded, then said, "Give me a minute, then you can follow me."

She had a few words with the tow truck driver, then returned to her car, nodded to me, and we followed her to Minton Street.

The body of a woman aged about forty was sitting propped up against the wall, her chin on her chest, arms at her side, hands palm up on the pavement.

It took only a quick look for Heather to identify her as Amy.

Doc Sheddon arrived five minutes after we did, seemingly full of beans despite the hour and the gathering crowd.

"Harry, m'boy," he said. "It's been a while, but here we are again. I'd say how nice it is to see you, but, under the circumstances, that would be a puerile observation, would it not?" And he beamed at me.

"Nice to see you, too, Doc," I said sarcastically, and stood to one side to let him do his thing. It didn't take him long to decide, from the body temperature and the lack of rigor, that she'd been dead between one and two hours. He also noticed a bruise to the left cheek and an injection site on the inside of her left arm.

"I can't say for certain, but I don't like the looks of it, Kate," he said when he rejoined us. "At first glance, and the needle close to her right hand, it would appear to be a self-induced overdose. But she received a blow to the face that would undoubtedly have incapacitated her, and, though I may be missing something, there are no other obvious signs of drug use, no track marks. I'll know more when I get her on the table, but it looks very much like a homicide to me. I'll do the post first thing tomorrow. You'll attend, Kate?" he asked.

"Yeah… No, I'll have Corbin do it," she replied.

"Then I'll have the body removed to the forensic center," he replied. "And I'll see Corbin bright and early." Then he turned to me and said, "Don't be a stranger, Harry." And, with that, he bustled away to the waiting paramedics.

"Well, that's a bummer," I said, staring down at the now supine body of Amy Murphy.

"That's a bit cold, don't you think?" Kate asked.

"Yeah… I suppose it is," I replied. Then I frowned and said, "By the way, where's Samson?"

"He's with Thomas," she replied. "I'd just gotten home when you called."

I nodded. "She'd been clean for more than fifteen years, Kate," I said.

"We'll see, Harry," she said. "I'll call you tomorrow when I know for sure."

I pursed my lips and stared at her.

"I know that look, Harry," she said, "and the answer's no. Stay out of it."

I nodded. She was right. I had enough on my plate. She had a team of detectives dedicated to such a case, and they were top-notch. I could only get in the way.

Even so, I left the scene that evening knowing in my gut that Amy Murphy's death was no accidental overdose. Nor was it a coincidence. I also found it strange that someone could have been keeping that close of an eye on her, that they knew she was about to talk and could have killed her in a matter of hours after Heather had spoken to her. Another coincidence? I didn't think so.

And so, reluctantly, I went home.

It was almost ten when I walked into the living room that evening. Jade was in bed, and Amanda was watching some off-the-wall gardening show.

"Oh dear," she said when she saw the look on my face. "What's wrong?" And I told her.

For me, it was the beginning of a ten-minute rant. I mean, I'd lost what I'd considered to be a potentially hot lead. If Amy had information that someone was willing to kill her for, to keep her from talking, it goes without saying that it could have broken the case wide open.

I was in bed at eleven that night, exhausted, and even though I had much on my mind, I had no trouble falling asleep. My last thought being, *I wonder if her death is a foretaste of what's to come.*

16

Again, I slept like a dead dog that night. I woke to the sound of my alarm at six-thirty to find an overnight text from Tim asking if I was coming into the office that morning as he thought he'd found something that might be helpful.

So, I decided to forego my usual morning run in favor of fifty laps in the pool. Then I showered, dressed quickly, inhaled a cup of coffee and some scrambled eggs and toast, and by eight o'clock was out the door and heading down the mountain into the city.

I arrived at my offices to find Tim in the lobby looking as if he'd slept in his clothes, which he probably had. Tim is a creature of the night, a nocturnal beast that inhabits the digital nether world like a prowling cat. I sometimes wonder if he ever sleeps.

"Tim," I said as I walked through the outer door. "You're looking… chipper this morning," I lied. "What d'you have for me?"

"Well, I—"

"Just one moment, kiddo," I said. "Coffee first, then show and tell."

He nodded and followed me like a whipped puppy to the

breakroom where I poured us both a mug of coffee. Jacque was already there.

"I'm callin' in a breakfast order," she said. "You want something?"

I did. I was still hungry, so I had her order a sausage and egg biscuit and an order of hash browns. Then I followed them both to the darkened room at the far end of the corridor that was his lair. The air within was warm and heavy. The only lights a single green banker's lamp and the glow generated by the six wide-screen monitors.

It was a place I didn't enjoy. I found it claustrophobic, cave-like, even, but Tim liked it, and that was all that mattered.

Tim sat down in front of the twin banks of monitors, made a few keystrokes, then pointed to the screen in front of him. "Lana Baudette," he said.

On the screen was an image of a woman dressed in an electric blue evening gown.

"That was taken three months ago at a breast cancer fundraiser," he said. "The guy with her is Charles Stewart."

He pointed at a second screen. "There she is in a group photo at the same event."

I leaned forward and looked at the group photo. It included seven women and four men. Lana was at the center of the photo.

"And there," he said, pointing at a third screen, "is an email string between Lana and someone called Starlight. As you can see, they're talking money. Apparently, Lana shorted her on a gig. Well, that's what they're calling it. I'm assuming Starlight's an escort. Lana's still in business. Anyway, as you can see, they seem to have sorted it out."

"So it seems," I said, thoughtfully, looking at the images. "I wonder who the men are. Can you find out? The women, too? Escorts maybe?"

"It might take a while," he said, "but I'm sure I can."

"Does she have a website?" I asked.

"Now that… I dunno. There's nothing on the web, but maybe the dark web. I haven't looked, but I will."

I nodded and said, "Good job, Tim. Keep it up. Now I need an address for Lana."

"Already texted it to your phone," he said, grinning up at me.

"Thanks," I said, then turned to Jacque and said, "TJ in yet?"

She nodded. "In his office," she replied.

"Good," I said. "Now all we need is that breakfast and we're out of here."

And, thirty-minutes later, we were. TJ and I were heading up Signal Mountain on Highway 127 to an address overlooking the river on the western slopes of the mountain.

The house, an old-build, half-timbered, half-mansion—possibly from the 1880s—was lovely and, knowing real estate prices on the mountain as I did, obviously worth a packet. Why wasn't I surprised?

I parked in front of the porch on the semi-circular drive, turned off the engine, looked at TJ and said, "You ready for this?"

"Should be a hoot," he said as he pushed open the car door and stepped out onto the drive.

We stepped up to the front door, and TJ pressed the doorbell button. The door was opened a moment later by a man who looked vaguely familiar. He was about my age, tall, aristocratic, dressed in tan slacks and a long sleeve, button-down shirt: open at the neck, cuffs turned back.

"Can I help you?" he asked.

"We'd like to talk to Mrs. Baudette," I said.

"Who are you?" the accent was southern, slightly clipped.

"I'm Harry Starke," I replied. "This is—"

"I know you," he said. "You're that private investigator. I've seen you on television. What do you want with my mother?"

"I'd like to ask her a few questions?" I replied.

"About what?" he asked haughtily.

"Oh, for God's sake, Arthur. Show them in," a woman's voice called.

"It seems mother will see you," he said, stepping aside. "If you'll wait just a moment, I'll take you to her."

My first thought was, *If she's your mother, who's the woman in the photo taken three months ago? She must be at least sixty.*

As it turned out, the photo did her proud. She might have been in her sixties, but she looked forty and, from what I could see, other than a little work on her neck, it was all her. Her skin was near perfect, though her face had that age-hardened look about it. Lips? As God made them. Breasts? A quick glance was all that was needed to see that they were all her own. She was wearing a white headband over her long platinum blonde hair and a flowing ice blue satin kaftan.

"Mr. Starke," she said, rising to her feet. "You're quite famous, aren't you? To what do I owe the honor?"

"Mrs. Baudette," I began. "This is my associate, TJ Bron. We're here to talk to you about Elizabeth Reynolds."

"Please, won't you sit down?" she said, waving a hand at an overstuffed antique sofa. "And it's Ms. I dropped the Mrs. a long time ago."

We sat down and so did she, folding her hands demurely in her lap.

"Elizabeth…" she said, paused, and then said, "That was so long ago. Why now?"

The voice was soft, almost lilting. It reminded me of Rosolynn Carter.

There's no point in beating around the bush, I thought.

"We think David Archer is innocent," I said.

She stared at me for a moment, a weird expression on her face, then she laughed and said, "Oh, dear Lord. But wasn't it you that put him away?"

And there it is again, I thought. *I'm going to have to get used to it, I guess, but what a pain in the ass having to explain it every time.*

"That's true," I said. "But new evidence has come to light—"

"Really?" she interjected, cutting me off. "What new evidence?"

"I'm afraid I'm not at—"

"Yes, yes, yes," she said, cutting me off again. "I've heard that spiel so many times. It's so very boring. Very well. What can I tell you that you don't already know?"

I glanced at the open doorway, where her son was hovering.

She caught my look. "You can go now, Arthur. I'll call if I need you. And please close the door, there's a good boy."

At that, I had to smile, though I quickly wiped it away.

"As I was saying," I said, "new evidence has come to light that we think will prove David Archer's innocence. Which is all to the good, but it also means that the killer is still out there, and we believe he's killed again."

That was a bit of a stretch. We still had no definitive proof that Amy Murphy was murdered, but what the hell?

"You were Elizabeth's employer," I continued. "D'you remember if she was worried about anything those last few days before she died? Did she mention anything? Was she being threatened?"

She bit her top lip and let it pop out, then shook her head slightly and said, "Not that I can recall, but then, she didn't confide in me, and it was so long ago. Even so, I think I would have remembered."

"I don't suppose you have a list of her clients?" I asked.

At that, she smiled. "Really, Mr. Starke… Or may I call you Harry? Mr. Starke seems so… formal, don't you think?"

"That would be fine," I replied, smiling back at her.

She batted her eyebrows, looked a little embarrassed, then

smiled again and said, "My family has been in the bordello business for a very long time, Harry, going all the way back to the Revolution, in fact. My great-great grandmother was the famous Ellie Duchamp. She ran Ellie's Place right here in Chattanooga. The bordello is a thing of the past, as you well know. But the family tradition lives on." She glanced at the door and sighed. "Though maybe not for much longer, I'm afraid," she said dryly. "Don't you find that interesting, Harry?"

"Yes, indeed," I replied, and I meant it.

"I don't keep client lists in my head, Harry, but I do have a wonderful memory. Over the three years Elizabeth worked for me, she saw a great many… clients, but only a few became regulars. She was a lovely girl, very pretty, thus she was able to demand the highest rates. She was very popular, but also very discerning. Charles Stewart," she said, thoughtfully, "the attorney was one. I still see him quite often, though not as a client. He has a lovely wife, you know? And there was Walter Jeffries, a very nice man; an accountant. Simian Woodley; he owns, or owned, a restaurant downtown. And there was Gregory Pitson; a mean little man, but he paid well. Some of the others are either out of state or they have passed away. Oh, and there was that policeman. I don't remember his name. Something Jewish, I think. That's all I can remember."

She tilted her head to one side, lowered it a little, and looked at me through her eyelashes.

"How about Councilman Keighley?" I asked. "Was he a client?"

"Walter?" she laughed. "Oh, dear me, no. He's a good friend. A philanthropist and a happily married man. Has been for more than thirty years."

"And you're sure she never mentioned anyone that… she was worried about, that frightened her, perhaps?"

"No, but as I said, she didn't confide in me."

"What about Amy Murphy?" I asked.

"What about her?" she replied.

"I—"

"She's dead," TJ said, cutting me off. "We think she was murdered last night. Harry was supposed to meet her. They found her body in an alley. The supposed victim of a self-inflicted overdose."

"What?" she gasped. Her face drained of its color. "That's not possible. She's clean. She has been for years. I saw her only two days ago. She was clean, and she was proud of it."

"You saw her?" I asked. "What was that about?"

"We're friends," she replied. "We go back a long way. We'd meet once a month for lunch. Usually on Tuesdays. She's dead?"

"She is," I said. "I'm sorry. It's obviously a great shock."

"What did you talk about?" TJ asked.

"Just… things," she said. "She was a friend. I've known her since… before Elizabeth was murdered. We talked about everyday things."

"Did you talk about Elizabeth Reynolds?" he asked.

She shook her head. "No. Never. Why would we?"

"Because she was Amy Murphy's friend," TJ snapped. "She was going to talk to Harry. Someone found out about it and shoved a needle in her arm."

I gave him a warning look and said, "D'you have any idea who might have wanted Amy out of the way, or who killed Elizabeth?"

Again, she shook her head. "Other than that Archer kid, no. Of course not," she replied.

"How d'you get your clients?" I asked.

She stared at me for a moment, then said, "Me? I'm retired. I have been for many years."

"Then who's running your business?" I said, pointedly.

"What business?" she asked, locking eyes with me.

I thought for a minute, then stood up and said, "Thank you for your time, Ms. Baudette. I think that will do for now. If you think of anything."

She remained seated. I handed her my card. She looked at it, then at me and said, "You're welcome, Harry. Please, come back… anytime." And she raised her eyebrows as if to further emphasize the suggestion.

"I may need to," I said as I heard the door open behind me. I turned to see her son standing in the opening, a smirk on his face. How did he do that? I wondered.

"Show them out, will you, Arthur?" she said with a wave of her hand.

Two minutes later, we were back out on the drive walking to the car. TJ was silent, though he did have a tiny smile on his lips.

"What?" I said, as I opened my car door.

"You still got it, Harry," he said, grinning. "That woman was flirting with you."

I would have denied it, but I'd noticed it myself, so I merely shrugged.

"What d'you make of all that?" he said as I started the engine.

I sat for a moment, thinking, then said, "I'm not sure, but there were a couple of things. One, I don't think she's retired and two, how old d'you think her son is?"

TJ shrugged. "Early forties?" he asked.

I nodded. "He would have been in his early twenties when Reynolds was murdered. Makes you think, doesn't it?"

TJ nodded slowly but didn't answer.

We were still parked in Baudette's drive. I put the car in drive, then put it back in park.

"I need to call Tim," I said and took out my phone.

"Tim," I said when he answered. "I have some names for you. Walter Jefferies. He's an accountant. And Simian Woodley. He used to own a restaurant downtown. And I want you to run

Arthur Baudette. He's Lana Baudette's son…" And then I had an epiphany. "See what you can find out about a bordello, Ellie's Place? Apparently, it was well known in the 1880s. See if you can find a reference to the name today, or in the last twenty-five years."

"Will do," he replied. "I should have something for you in an hour, maybe two."

"No great rush," I said. "This afternoon will do fine. Tell Jacque I should be back in about thirty minutes."

I hung up, put the car in drive, and we headed back down the mountain.

And then my phone rang. I glanced at the screen. It was Kate.

"Hey, Kate. What's up?"

"Can we meet?" she asked. "How about you buy me lunch?"

"Sure," I replied. "You have something for me?"

"Maybe," she replied.

"Okay," I said. "I'm on my way back to the office. I'll meet you in, say… an hour. Where?"

"How about that diner on Rossville Boulevard?"

I frowned. "Er, that's—"

"I know," she said, "but I'm going to be over that way, so it's handy."

"Well, okay then. See you in an hour."

17

THE DINER ON ROSSVILLE BOULEVARD WASN'T THE PLACE YOU'D want to take your wife or girlfriend, but they made the best burger in town, which is what I ordered when I met Kate for lunch that Thursday afternoon.

"So," I said after the server had taken our orders. "What's so urgent, and why here? I can think of better places."

We were seated facing each other in a booth by the window.

She narrowed her eyes, then looked at me and said, "Well, for one thing, Doc called me. And I just talked to Corbin. Apparently, Amy Murphy died of a massive overdose of a mixture of fentanyl and xylazine. She must have died within minutes. She also sustained a blow to the left side of her head, which Doc thinks would have rendered her unconscious, so she probably wouldn't have suffered."

"Xylazine, huh?" I said. "That's a tranquilizer. They call it tranq, right?"

She nodded. "It's an animal tranquilizer. Mixed with fentanyl, it can be deadly."

I heaved a sigh. "So you think it was a homicide, then?"

"Doc seems to think so," she said.

"Time of death?" I asked.

"Between five and six," she replied.

"She was supposed to meet me at six," I said. "It can't be a coincidence. You know she'd been clean for more than fifteen years?"

"Doc said there were no signs of regular use," she replied. "Any idea who might have wanted her dead?"

I shook my head. "Someone who didn't want her talking to me, I guess. But who? I have no idea. I have some names but nothing solid. I've already talked to several people, including retired Sergeant Tom Miller and your old pal Henry. They were both involved with Reynolds, though they deny any wrongdoing."

"Why does that not surprise me?" she said. "Who else did you talk to?"

"Just Lana Baudette," I replied. "I was on my way back from her place when you called. Interesting, to say the least. She gave me a couple of names, and she has a son, Arthur, that was about the right age when Reynolds was killed. Strange cat. Creeps about like a frickin' ghost. I've got Tim checking him out."

She grimaced, took a swallow of her coffee, then said, "I'm worried about this Amy Murphy thing. You're right. It can't be a coincidence. It also means you could be the killer's next target."

I stared at her for a moment. I hadn't thought of that. She was right, though.

"You should be careful, Harry."

I nodded, thinking about it. Wondering who the hell it could be, and I came up with nothing.

"I don't think it would be anyone I've already talked to," I said. "Miller's an ornery old cuss, but I'm not getting that kind of vibe from him. Henry…" I smiled at the idea. "He doesn't have it in him either. Lana Baudette?" I shook my head. "Her son, maybe, but again, I'm not feeling it."

"That gut of yours is going to get you killed one of these days," Kate said dryly. "What about the other names you have?"

"Charlie Stewart. The attorney," I replied. "We both know him. I don't see it, but maybe he knows something."

She nodded. "Who else?"

"Walter Jefferies. He's an accountant, and Simian Woodley. He used to own Tankers on Georgia Avenue until it went out of business. I don't know either of them."

"Me neither," she said. "Anyone else?"

"Greg Pitson," I said, grinning across the table at her.

"Ah-hah," she said. "Now there's a name to conjure with. Nasty little man. A loan shark!"

"Technically, he operates a couple of payday loan shops," I said.

"Okay, good one," she said. "He's just down the road a piece. How about we go talk to him when we're done here?"

"Are you sure you want to do that?" I asked.

"Why wouldn't I be?" she asked.

"Well… It's an active investigation. Yours is," I said.

"So?" she asked, smiling.

"Well, I'm not sure I'm comfortable with—"

"I can fix that," she said, cutting me off and taking out her phone.

She hit the speed dial and waited for an answer. It came almost immediately.

"Chief," she said, "I'm with Harry Starke… Yes, I know… What? Well, yeah… No. We're basically working the same case. I was hoping I could bring him in as a consultant." And with that, I shook my head and held up my hand. She ignored me. "No, Chief… Well, there's no sense in us tripping over each other and he… Yes, Chief… Yes, Chief… Yes, Chief… Got it. Yep… Goes without saying. Thank you, Chief." And she hung up, grinned at me and said, "Now it's official. You and your team are on my team. Ain't that grand?"

At first thought I didn't think it was so grand. On second thought, though, it did give me access to the PD and all its resources.

I just sat there staring at her, shaking my head.

"You really are something else, Kate," I said.

"Oh, come on, Harry," she said. "You know you love it. And it's not like it's the first time."

She was right about that. She'd hauled me in on… how many cases? I'd lost count.

"I'd like it a whole lot better if I was getting paid," I said caustically. "I need to call Jacque and let her know what's going on." Which I did.

Jacque wasn't pleased. She, too, didn't like us working for nothing.

I listened to her while she unloaded, then told her we were going to see Pitson, which didn't placate her one bit.

"Think about it, Jacque," I said. "Maybe working with Kate will speed things up a bit and we can be done with it."

"Well, there's dat, I suppose, but you better keep me in the loop, Harry Starke. Dat's all I can say." And with that, she hung up.

Kate, who'd heard most of the conversation, said, "Good Lord, Harry. You two are like an old married couple."

"What?" I asked.

"You heard," she said. "Are you like that with Amanda?" I didn't quite know how to take what she was saying, but then, seeing the grin, I realized she was joking.

"She's my partner," I said, a little self-consciously. "We discuss… things."

"Come on," she said. "Eat up and let's go see Pitson. It should be fun."

And we did!

18

GREG PITSON WAS... AN ANOMALY; STILL IS. HE'S A FINANCIAL wizard. He's also a crook. He began his career early while still in high school. He loaned money—small amounts—to fellow students at exorbitant interest rates. Where he learned it, nobody to my knowledge knows. By the time he graduated, he was reputed to be worth in excess of twenty-five thousand and, like any good citizen, he was paying his taxes on time. He carried on his lending throughout his college years and, by the time he graduated, he was quite a wealthy young man. He'd also garnered a reputation as a brute. You borrowed money from him, you'd better pay it back on time, or else.

With the proceeds of his college enterprise, he was able to open his first payday loan store by the time he was twenty-five, and a second one a year later. In 2021, at the time all this was taking place, he'd become an extremely wealthy man and had made some very unsavory friends.

He was fifty-four years old, married with two children, both girls, aged twenty-seven and twenty-nine. Jennifer, the oldest, worked in the shop on Rossville Boulevard.

I'd never had anything to do with him, but I knew him by

reputation as a hard, unforgiving businessman, not afraid to break a finger or two when he deemed it necessary. He was not a man you'd want to cross.

Kate and I walked into his shop that afternoon to find it deserted except for the young woman behind the counter.

"Good afternoon," she said, smiling. "How can I help you today?"

"We'd like to see Mr. Pitson," Kate said, showing her badge, at which the woman visibly blanched.

"Do you have an appointment?" she asked hesitantly.

"I don't need an appointment," Kate said, smiling. "Just tell him Captain Gazzara with the Chattanooga Police Department would like a word."

She hesitated for a moment, then picked up the phone and did as she was asked.

"He'll be with you in a minute," she said. "He said for you to take a seat."

There was a row of chairs set back against the front window. Kate sat down. I preferred to stand, reluctant to put my back to the window.

He arrived a few minutes later, looked appraisingly at Kate, then, without a word, motioned for us to follow him.

Pitson was a small man, thin, with a thin face and receding hair. His dark brown eyes were set just a little too close together.

He took us back to an office that belied his wealth. The furniture was top quality but old: a mahogany desk, three high-back chairs, a leather couch set against the wall opposite his desk, a credenza behind his desk and a bank of steel file cabinets against the wall opposite the door.

The light was dim, the atmosphere heavy, silence reigned.

He looked at Kate, or should I say he ogled her, then he looked at me and said, "I know her. Who are you?"

"He's a colleague," Kate answered for me. "This is Mr. Harry Starke."

"Is he now?" he asked as he sat down behind his desk. "Well, sit yourselves down, unless you prefer to stand, that is. What is it you want of me?"

"How well did you know Elizabeth Reynolds?" I asked.

"Who?" He frowned, looking genuinely puzzled, and then he caught on. "Oh yes. I remember," he said, "Liz. Nice girl. Shame what happened to her. I knew her quite well, as you probably know…" He paused, looking at me, then said, "Say, aren't you the cop that put that boy away? Solved it pretty damn quick, if I remember correctly."

I nodded. "It was a long time ago. I'm not a cop anymore. Where were you that night, the night she was killed? D'you remember?"

"Actually, surprisingly I do," he replied. "I remember because I was in Las Vegas, and I got a call from Lana telling me all about it. You know Lana, don't you? Anyway, I remember thinking it was a damn good job I was where I was. I even kept the hotel receipt. It might take a while, but I can dig it out, if you like."

"We'd appreciate that," Kate said. "When can I have it?"

"As I said, it might take a while. Shall we say tomorrow, in the afternoon? I'll have someone deliver it to you."

"What was your relationship with Elizabeth?" I asked.

He looked at me, obviously taken aback, then said, "She was an escort. What d'you think my relationship with her was? I was a client. Is that not enough for you?"

"So you knew her quite well, then?"

"Yes, I knew her quite well," he replied impatiently. "Didn't I already tell you that?"

"Did she ever talk about her clients?" Kate asked.

"Not to me," he replied, "and if she had, I would have

dropped her. If she would talk about others, she would talk about me."

"When did you last see her?" I asked.

He shrugged, then said, "Now that is a little more difficult. Two, three weeks before she died, perhaps. I'm not sure."

"Did she seem worried about anything?" I asked.

"Not that I can remember."

"What about Amy Murphy?" Kate asked.

Again, he looked taken aback. "Amy? What about her?"

"You knew her?" Kate asked.

"Yes, I knew her. So what?"

"She's dead," Kate said. "Murdered. Last night."

He looked stunned. "What?"

"She was murdered," Kate said. "Someone pumped her full of xylazine."

I glanced at Kate. She was watching him closely. He was slowly shaking his head.

"What was your relationship with her?" Kate asked.

"She was a friend," he replied. "I've known her for years. She was one of Liz's friends."

"She was also an escort," Kate said.

"Yes, she was," he replied.

"Were you one of her clients?" Kate asked.

"No!" he snapped, then thought better of it. "Well, it depends on what you mean by client. I saw her a couple of times, professionally, and we got along. She was fun. And… look, she was nice. We kept in touch over the years."

"When did you last see her?" I asked.

He looked at me, then at Kate, then shook his head and said, "I dunno. It's been a while. A couple of months ago maybe."

"Where were you between six and seven last night, Mr. Pitson?" Kate asked.

"I was here," he said. "We don't close till seven. Margie was here. She can confirm it."

"Did she, by any chance, owe you money, Mr. Pitson?" I asked.

He frowned, then said, "A little. She had a payday loan. It was just renewed. She paid on time, if that's what you're asking."

I wasn't impressed. His alibis meant nothing. I knew for a fact he had two low-level goons on his payroll. He could easily have ordered a hit on either woman, but why would he?

"How well d'you know Lana Baudette?" Kate asked.

He shrugged. "I don't. Not anymore. Haven't seen the woman in years… Look, I realize you have a job to do, but why me? Surely you don't think I had anything to do with the deaths of either of these two women?"

"As you say," Kate replied. "We have a job to do. We're talking to anyone that knew them or availed themselves of their services. Your name came up several times. So here we are."

He sighed, then said, "I understand. So, are we done?"

"Not quite," Kate said. "Who else was seeing them that you know of?"

He immediately shook his head and said, "I wasn't privy to that kind of information, Captain. They didn't talk about their clients, and I didn't ask." Then he looked at me and said, "You were in charge of the investigation into Liz's death. Why didn't you talk to me then?"

Kate looked at me as I considered my answer. "Things were a little different back then," I said. "We had all the evidence we needed to close the case, and we did. A jury agreed." It was weak. I knew it and so did he, as evidenced by the sly smile on his mean little mouth.

"And now you think you sent an innocent man away for life," he said. "Way to go, Mr. Starke."

There was no answer to that, so I didn't bother. Fortunately,

Kate could see what was going on and brought the interview to a close.

She stood up, dropped her card on his desk and said, "Thank you for your time, Mr. Pitson. If you think of anything else, please call me."

He, too, stood up. "It's been a pleasure, Captain. And yes, of course, if I remember anything, I'll call you."

And with that, we left him staring after us, smirking.

Kate stopped by the desk and talked to Margie for a few moments, then joined me outside.

"She confirms he was here till almost eight last night," she said.

"Well, that was something; the interview," I said as we walked to our cars.

"No more than I expected," Kate said. "What now?"

"Let's go back to my place," I said without thinking.

"Why, Harry Starke, you're a married man," she replied, smiling.

"Get over it," I said, grinning at her. "You know what I meant. I need to bring my team up to speed, now that you're on board and—"

"Me? On board?" she said, interrupting me. "It's the other way around, I think, but I get it. Why don't I have Corbin join us?"

"Sounds like a plan," I said.

19

Twenty minutes later, we were back at my offices, in the breakroom pouring coffee. Jacque handed me a list of calls for me to handle, all of which I ignored, much to her consternation.

"Get everyone together in the conference room, including you, please," I said. "Corbin will be here soon. Have Lucy show him through when he arrives. I'll join you ASAP. I just need a few minutes."

She nodded, and I went upstairs to my office. It wasn't that I had anything to do. I just needed a few minutes of quiet time to gather my thoughts. I scrabbled through the sheets of notes on my desk and made what I intended to be a short list of pertinent questions that I thought needed to be answered. By the time I'd finished—not more than five minutes later—I was horrified by how long the list was.

I sat back in my chair, laid my head back, and stared up at the chandelier, wondering what the hell I'd gotten myself into. I tried to make sense of it all, but, in the end, I gave up, just as Jacque called to say everyone was waiting, including Kate's partner, Corbin Russell. And so, I scraped it all together, pushed it to one side, grabbed my list and a notebook and headed down to the conference room.

"Good afternoon, everyone," I said as I entered the room and took my seat at the head of the table. "Sorry to keep you waiting. Corbin. Nice to see you. Before we begin, does anyone have anything they'd like to say?"

No one did, so I began.

"First, I'd like to welcome Kate and Corbin. As you know, Kate has insisted on roping us into the Amy Murphy investigation, which, we are both reasonably sure, is linked to the murder of Elizabeth Reynolds."

I paused, looked around the table, and then continued, "Having said that, I have a gnawing feeling that we—perhaps I should say I—have bitten off more than we can chew. This investigation seems to have taken on a life of its own. It involves a senior police officer, possibly two, and a collection of Chattanooga's most prominent citizens. Not good! So, what do we know so far?"

And I proceeded to review the events of the previous several days, beginning with Betty Markham's visit and ending with the Pitson interview.

"My feeling is," I continued, "Henry Finkle and Tom Miller were both involved with Reynolds. Tom was having sex with her in return for protection, but he wasn't taking money. Finkle…" I sighed, shook my head, and continued, "Probably both, though, in both cases, it's just a gut feeling. It's also a gut feeling that neither of them had anything to do with her death."

I looked briefly at my notes. "Now for Pitson. He has an alibi for both murders and so would appear to be in the clear, but, as I mentioned to Kate, he employs a couple of heavies, so we can't eliminate him.

"Tim," I continued, "I gave you a list. How are you doing with it?"

"Well, I..." He did that thing with his glasses and then continued, "I sent you a breakdown. You should have it on your phone. I—"

"Why don't you just do a quick run-through so we all know what's going on and can make suggestions?" I said.

He nodded, swallowed, looked at me and then said, "Well, you've already spoken to three of them but, short story, their financials are, Pitson: net worth is estimated to be in excess of seventeen-point-two million—"

TJ whistled, interrupting him. He gave TJ a withering look and then continued, "not counting what he has tucked away in three offshore accounts. One is in Bermuda. The other two are in the Caymans. He has one arrest for extortion, but the charges were dropped for lack of evidence. Other than that, he's clean."

"Geez, I wish I was that clean," TJ said. "Seventeen mill. Who was it said crime doesn't pay? He sure as hell had that wrong."

"All right," I said. "That's enough. Continue, Tim."

"Captain Henry Finkle's net worth is estimated to be six-hundred-thirty-three thousand. He has one-hundred-ninety thousand in outstanding debt, including his mortgage of one-hundred-eleven thousand. He also has a car payment of five-sixty a month. His credit score is seven-twenty. He has no criminal record, obviously, but he does have several internal reprimands on his personal record, and he was demoted from assistant chief to captain after an extensive IA investigation following allegations of sexual harassment." He looked at Kate over the top of his glasses and grinned at her. She ignored him, though I knew she knew exactly what he was getting at.

"Thomas Miller," Tim continued. "Retired detective sergeant. Net worth four-hundred-twenty-two thousand. No mortgage. No debts other than two credit cards totaling three-thousand-two-hundred, twenty-one dollars. Five commendations.

Unblemished record. A fine officer by any standard, I would say."

He looked up and beamed around the room.

Kate sat back in her chair and folded her arms. Corbin continued biting the knuckle of the forefinger of his left hand. TJ looked bored. Heather was writing in a notebook, taking copious notes, as usual. Jacque looked plaintively at me as if to say, please spare me from this ordeal. But I just smiled at her and Tim continued.

"You asked me to look into Arthur Baudette, Walter Jeffries, Simian Woodley, and Walter Keighley. At first glance, they all appear to be fine, upstanding individuals, though Baudette is a bit of an anomaly. He's never worked, as far as I can tell. He has no debt. He doesn't even have a bank account. When I ran his social, all that came up was his mother's address. He has no social media presence, and he doesn't have a police record. If he'd been anyone else, I'd have said he's a ghost. It's strange as hell if you ask me."

"Perhaps he doesn't need any of that," Corbin said. "I know the type. He sounds like a momma's boy. She provides everything, including girls, I shouldn't wonder."

Tim shrugged and continued, "Walter Jeffries, Simian Woodley, and Walter Keighley. I can't find anything untoward on any of them. Jeffries is a successful accountant. Woodley retired from the restaurant business in 2010. Keighley is a respected councilman. None of them have records."

He coughed, picked up his coffee mug, took a sip, swallowed, put the cup down again, then put a finger to his glasses and said, "Charles Stewart, attorney at law. Much the same as the others. I could find nothing that would make him a suspect other than he was a client of Elizabeth Reynolds, right?"

He looked at me and I nodded and looked at Kate and said, "Might be worth taking a look at him next. What d'you think?"

She nodded and looked at Corbin. He shrugged but said nothing.

"Did you get a chance to look at Assistant Chief Gordon Whacker?" I asked, catching the sharp look from Kate.

Tim frowned and made a face. "You didn't say anything about a police chief."

"Tim," I said. "I… meant to. Sorry." I turned to look at Kate and said, "What about Whacker, Kate? We know he was seeing Reynolds. We need to talk to him."

"I think I'd better handle him," she said. "And I'd better run it by Johnston first. Knowing Whacker as I do, he's going to be pissed."

"I'd like to be present," I said. "Reynolds is my investigation. I would have interviewed him with or without you."

"As I said," she said, dryly. "I'll run it by the chief. If he agrees, all well and good."

"If he doesn't, I'll do it anyway," I replied. "That's why I left the force; I don't have to play by those rules anymore. If you can fix it, fine. If not, I will."

"Hey, Harry," Corbin said. "There's no need to take that attitude. We have to live with the consequences. You don't."

"It's all right, Corbin," Kate said, putting a hand on his arm. Then said, "Harry, I get it. You want a result. But you're rushing it, just as you did in 2001. It's going to take time. We're chasing down leads from twenty-plus years ago. It's what I do. Patience is the key here. It's more than likely going to take someone coming forward with new information to crack it. But here it is as I see it. I know how this is going to sound, but we have to look upon the murder of Amy Murphy as a plus. We know the two cases have to be connected, which means Reynolds' killer is still out there, and he, or she, knows we're close and is panicking. And my guess is, they're going to make a mistake."

I listened to what Kate said, and I couldn't help but agree with her, but it was my contention that the killer was somebody we already knew. Somebody who had access to information at the highest levels. That, to me, spelled Whacker.

"I agree," I said, "but I still want a face-to-face with Whacker. It's been less than a week since Betty Markham walked into this office, and we've already lost a potentially key witness. You're right, Kate. The killer's panicking, but we still have no idea who it is. We have a half-dozen suspects yet to clear and one of them is an assistant police chief. He has to be a priority."

She nodded, sat forward, and leaned her elbows on the table. "And I agree," she said. "But you must let me do this. Corbin's right. We have to live with it. You don't. You'll be there when I interview him. I promise."

I nodded. What else could I do?

I looked at Tim and said, "Bob Williams? MaryAnn's husband. What've you got?"

"Nothing of note," he replied, nervously, unable to make eye contact with me. "As far as I can tell, he's clean." Then he looked up at me and said, "I do have something you'll be interested in, though. That bordello you mentioned. There's a website, local, Ellie's Place dot com, and guess what? It's a hookup site. I haven't figured out who's running it yet, but it looks promising. You want to see?"

"Yeah, I want to see," I replied. "Show me."

The website was… a sophisticated, well-designed shopfront for a collection of classy men and women for hire, ostensibly as escorts for upscale functions and the like, with a note that services and fees were negotiable.

The women each had a page, or several pages, of their own where their wares were on show. All were quite beautiful and were wearing evening gowns. Those that had multiple pages showed off their attributes, posing in bikinis, sportswear, or engaged in outdoor activities. The ladies were available for an evening or an extended period, depending on the punter's needs or desires.

The gentlemen, for that's how they were described, were all rugged-looking individuals and were also dressed to sell: white or black tie, business suits, swimwear and, of course, sportswear.

I flipped through the pages— more than a hundred— impressed by the professionalism of the presentation. There was no mention of price or sexual services, but subtleties in the accompanying texts left little doubt that this was indeed a "hookup" site.

It was all good stuff, but of what use it would be, I couldn't see, not until I happened upon Starlight's listing.

Page one was headed, Starlight, in large, flowing silver text, and a photograph, an outdoor shot, taken in a flower garden, of a tall, sophisticated blonde wearing a form-fitting, silver evening gown. She was standing with a man wearing a black suit. She was facing the camera. He had his back to the camera. Her arm was on his shoulder. The image was obviously all about her and shot the way it was to emphasize her height. She was wearing heels and was a good half-a-head taller than the man. It was impressive, as were the next five pages showing her in hiking gear, a silver bikini, posing on a ten-meter diving board, playing tennis and, of course, at the wheel of a sailboat, laughing, her hair blowing in the wind.

The website blurb described her as a sophisticated, fun-loving, outdoorsy heterosexual female, age forty-four… And that's what got my attention. If she was forty-four now, that would make her twenty-three when Elizabeth was murdered. Was she an escort then? If so, did she know Elizabeth? And if she did, what could she tell us?

"Tim," I said without looking away from the screen. "We need to find out who this woman is. I want to talk to her."

"I thought that one would get your attention," he said.

I looked up at him. He was smiling.

"Her name is Janice Soames," he said, putting a slip of paper down on the table in front of me. "That's her address and cell number."

I looked up at him and shook my head. He never ceased to amaze me.

"Good job, Tim," I said. "Thank you." Then I looked at my watch. It was almost five-thirty.

"Okay," I said. "It's time to call it a day. So, to recap; Kate, you and I will talk to Stewart tomorrow morning. Jacque, it's late, but give him a call and see if you can set up an appointment. If you can't get ahold of him today, try again first thing in the morning. Kate, I'll let you know as soon as I know something. I'll call August this evening and see what he knows about him."

I thought for a moment, then said, "Kate, you'll see what you can do regarding Whacker, yes?"

She nodded.

"TJ, Heather," I said. "I want you to interview Simian Woodley and Walter Jeffries." They both nodded. Heather wrote something in her notebook.

"That leaves Janice Soames, Bob Williams, Shirley Castle's husband Chester, and Councilman Walter Keighley. We want to know where Williams was while MaryAnn was with David Archer. In other words, does he have an alibi for the hours nine until eleven?"

I looked around the table. They were all making notes except Kate, who still had her arms folded.

"Okay!" I said. "Those are the rest of the names we know who had contact either with Elizabeth Reynolds or Lana Baudette or both. If they're suspects in the Reynolds case, they are, by default, suspects in the murder of Amy Murphy. We need to talk to them, soonest. I want to talk to Soames…" I looked at Kate, my eyebrows raised in question. She nodded.

"That leaves three," I said, and I again looked at Kate.

Kate turned her head, looked at her partner and said, "Corbin, you can organize that. Put Tracey and Cooper on two of them. You and Hawk take the other one. Figure who gets who between you and let me know your game plan."

Corbin finished scribbling, then looked at Kate and nodded, then at me and winked.

"That it, then?" Kate asked, rising to her feet.

I thought for a moment and then said, "Yes. That will do it for today. Jacque, I'll see you here at eight-thirty. The rest of my people, you know what to do tomorrow. We'll meet back here tomorrow afternoon. Kate, I'll call you. Okay?"

She nodded, told everyone to have a good evening, and then she and Corbin left.

Me? I spent a few minutes with Jacque and then I left, too.

~

It was almost six o'clock when I turned off Broad onto Lee Highway. I was… a little worse for wear, tired, irritable and frustrated. So it's not really surprising that I missed what was going on behind me.

I made the left onto Scenic Highway, rounded the sharp left-hand bend and was proceeding up the mountain when I glanced into my driver's side mirror and noticed a black SUV closing quickly. I didn't think anything of it until I reached Craven's Terrace, where I pulled over to let it pass, which it did and disappeared on up the mountain at a dangerous speed.

I pulled out again and continued my leisurely drive home, past the Mountain Memories Souvenir Shop, where I noticed the SUV in the parking lot. Again, I thought nothing of it until, maybe five-hundred yards on, there it was again, on my tail, flashing its lights.

What the hell? I thought and pulled over in one of the pull offs and the big car roared by. The windows were heavily tinted, so I couldn't see the driver. I swore to myself and drove on up the mountain. I saw no more of the SUV and arrived home at six-thirty to a flailing of tiny arms and a flurry of kisses.

"Yay, Daddy's home," Jade yelled at the top of her voice. "Now, can we eat dinner? I'm hungry."

20

I THOUGHT NO MORE ABOUT THE SUV, PUTTING IT DOWN TO AN impatient driver with an ax to grind. Instead, I carried Jade into the house, popped her down on her feet, took the glass of Laphroaig from Amanda, and took a large swallow. The effect was almost instantaneous. I literally and visibly relaxed.

We sat down to a dinner of chicken in gravy over rice, followed by my favorite peach cobbler. Simple, but oh so satisfying.

It was just after seven-thirty when we finished dinner; late for me, and certainly late for Jade. So we hustled her off to bed, and I read her two short stories about Mr. Snickers, an arrogant and implausibly intelligent cat, and then I tucked her in, kissed her goodnight and went down to join Amanda pool-side.

By then, it was getting on towards eight and already dark outside. The weather, though, was still balmy, and the temperature was in the high sixties. The patio lights were on, as were the pool lights, and the city lights, some two-thousand feet below, were spread out like a glittering jeweled carpet; the great river, the Tennessee, a glittering band of silver. It was one of those memorable nights when you're glad to be alive.

Amanda was sitting on the low wall, glass in hand, bare feet dangling over the ten-foot drop to the landscaped slopes below, a small round tray at her side with a bottle of Riesling in a bucket of ice and a second glass thereon.

I stepped up behind her, put both hands on her shoulders and kneaded them.

"Hey," she whispered. "Come sit with me. It's so beautiful." And I did.

She put her glass down on the wall at her side, filled the spare, handed it to me and said, "Thank you, Harry." Then she leaned over and kissed me.

"What was that for?" I asked, smiling.

"Oh, I don't know," she replied, staring out over the city. "Everything, I suppose. Jade, of course. This…" She raised her glass to the city. "…our lives together… everything."

"You're maudlin tonight," I said as I sipped the ice cold wine.

She looked at me, smiled, shook her head, and said, "Not at all. Just thankful, is all. D'you remember when we first met, Harry? You were still with Kate. Who would have thought it would have turned out like this?"

"As I remember it," I said, "you hated my guts. That was a real hatchet job you did on me."

"Got your attention, though, didn't it?" She turned to look at me, smiling. "And no, I didn't hate your guts. I was just doing my job."

I leaned in and kissed her. "You sure as hell led me on a merry chase those first two years," I said.

"But I let you catch me, in the end," she said. The smile had turned into a grin. "But OMG, it's been one heck of a wild ride. Harry, I shot that woman to death; Calaway Jones." She was serious now. "I dream about that," she said. It was something she'd never mentioned before.

"Really?" I asked, frowning.

"Of course I do," she replied. "I shot her, Harry. Six times. I can still see her face… her eyes. It was awful."

"Not for me," I said. "She was about to brain me with a hunk of iron pipe. You saved my life. Had you and Tim not arrived when you did…" I didn't bother to finish.

"I know, but still…" and she began to cry.

I hastily grabbed the tray and moved it to my other side, then I took her in my arms and held her close. She sobbed into my shoulder.

"How many more times, Harry?" she whispered. "How many more times until…" She took a long shuddering breath, then looked up at me and said, "Bob saved your life twice, Kate at least once. Me, once. TJ twice. It's got to stop, Harry. I don't know how much more I can take."

And it was at that moment that I came to a decision.

I took a deep breath, squeezed her tight, and said, "You're right, Amanda. Of course you are, and I'm sorry I put you through it. After I close this one, I'll step away. We'll go on a long vacation. Jacque can run the company; she already does. I don't know what I'll do, but I can't keep on putting you and Jade through this. It seems like I'm a magnet for trouble."

She pushed back from me, her hands on my chest, looked up at me, her cheeks wet, and smiled. "That's a lovely thought," she said. "And I appreciate it more than you'll ever know, but I'm not going to hold you to it. You'll always be you, and I wouldn't have it any other way. You'd be miserable if you didn't have your work. Now…" She pushed away from me, "let's talk no more about it. Let's just enjoy the evening and each other… I want you to make love to me. Right now. Out here. Under the stars."

And I did. And once again, I was glad to be alive.

But I didn't sleep well that night. My conversation with Amanda whirled around in my mind, and I was haunted by the monsters that inhabited the dark corners of the bedroom. Childish,

I know, but they haunted me when I was a child, and they seemed to return whenever I was in trouble. Were they a portent of things to come, of impending doom? I didn't know then and I don't know now. But, over the years, I'd come to regard them as part of my inner workings: the monsters, my gut. Kate once told me I was psychic, that I have second sight. I'd laughed at her, but sometimes I wondered, and, as I lay there staring up into the dark corners of the room, I actually shuddered.

It turned out to be a long night. I did get a little sleep but woke early at five.

Unwilling to lie there tossing and turning and disturbing Amanda, I rose, dressed in running gear, put on a headset, and set out on East Brow, heading south toward Georgia. I ran a little more than seven miles that morning, returning invigorated at six-thirty.

Amanda was already up and in the kitchen. I showered, dressed in my usual jeans, white shirt, no tie, and carried my blue suit jacket down to the kitchen and draped it over the back of a chair. Then I stepped up behind Amanda, slipped my arms around her waist, kissed her bare neck, and said, "Sleep well?"

"Yes," she lied. "You?"

"Like a dead dog," I lied.

"Liar," she said. "I was awake when you left, and I didn't go back to sleep."

"Geez, I'm sorry," I said and kissed her neck again.

"Coffee?" she asked.

"What do you think?" I asked.

"Scrambled eggs, bacon, and grits," she stated as she poured the coffee.

"Sounds good to me," I said as she handed me the steaming cup of inky black liquid.

I took it to the table and sat down.

"Maria will be here at seven-thirty," she said.

"Isn't she always?" I asked.

She nodded and put the plate down in front of me. "Four eggs lightly scrambled, three strips of bacon, and cheesy grits, just the way you like them."

"Wonderful," I said. "Thank you… Amanda, about last night—"

"Harry, stop," she said, putting a hand on my shoulder. "Last night was special. Don't spoil it."

"But—"

"I said stop," she said. "What we said to each other was a wonderful dream, no more than that. Life will go on, as it always does. I love you. I love you even more for what you said, and I know you meant it, but it was one fleeting moment. If I made you keep that promise, it would be the end of the Harry Starke I know and love, so thank you for the moment. Now, eat your breakfast."

What could I say? I could think of nothing then, and I can think of nothing now. So I said nothing.

21

It was a little before eight-thirty when I arrived at the office that morning to find Jacque and the gang already waiting for me.

Jacque and I drank a cup of coffee together—no, I didn't mention my promise to Amanda—and then we got down to it.

I asked her if she'd called Stewart. She hadn't. She said it was too early, but, at a little after nine, she did, and an appointment was made for ten-thirty that morning.

That done, I called Kate and arranged to pick her up at the police department at ten.

"By the way," Jacque said as we walked to her office, "what did August have to say about Stewart?"

I stopped walking. I'd completely forgotten to call him.

"You forgot, didn't you?" she said.

"Yeah, I did," I said as I looked at my watch. It was nine-fifteen. "I'll do it now."

"Dad," I said when he answered. "I have a quick question. What do you know about Charles Stewart?"

"That's a quick question that requires a long answer," he replied. "Why do you want to know?"

"He's a person of interest," I said.

"He's a defense attorney," August said, "and, as such, I know little about him other than he has an excellent reputation."

"Is he… is there … anything, any rumors, that he might be… shall we say—"

"Oh, for Heaven's sake, Harry," he said, cutting me off. "You would have made a lousy lawyer. If you're asking me if he's dirty, the answer, as far as I know, is no. Now, I have to go. I'm taking a deposition this morning and I don't want to be late. Is there anything else?"

"No, Dad. Thank you. See you on Sunday. Have a good day." And I hung up.

Jacque looked at me, smiling. "I heard dat," she said. "He's right, you would have made a terrible attorney. But you are an amazing investigator."

"Yeah, right," I said, wryly. "I'm outta here. Stay in touch with the others. Call me if anything comes up."

"Of course, boss," she said, grinning.

"Don't call me that," I said over my shoulder as I walked out the door.

I called Kate and told her I was on my way, and she was waiting for me out front when I arrived five minutes later.

"No Samson today?" I asked.

"No, Thomas has him," she said as she pulled the car door closed.

"That's getting to be a regular thing," I said. "I thought you and Samson were inseparable."

"We are, usually," she replied. "I'll pick him up later. Good night?" she asked as I pulled out onto Amnicola, heading toward downtown.

"Did I sleep well?" I said. "No."

"That's not what I meant," she said. "What I meant was, did you have a pleasant evening with your family?"

I thought about that before I answered, then said, "Yes. Amanda and I spent a pleasant evening together under the stars." I glanced at her. She was staring ahead, frowning.

"Sounds like one of those 'come to Jesus' moments," she said after a moment. "You want to talk about it?"

"How do you do that?" I said as I made the turn onto Lindsey.

"Do what?" she asked.

"Read my mind."

"You are an open book," she said. "What did you do? Make empty promises, again?"

"No… Yeah, sort of," I replied. "I told Amanda I'd quit after this one."

"Did you mean it? She asked.

"At the time… In the moment… I did. I still do."

"But?' she asked.

"Eh, it's difficult. I'm not yet fifty. It seems… I dunno."

"Does Amanda know how you feel?" she asked.

"I think so," I replied, "but you know her. She's hard to read sometimes."

"She deserves better, Harry," Kate said. "She's stood by you through a nightmare of a life. But you'll never stop. It's who you are."

I didn't answer that. One, because we'd reached our destination, and two, I didn't know how to.

Charles Stewart—Charlie to his friends, as he told me as we shook hands—was one of those confident, well-heeled, superbly dressed, slick attorneys I hate to deal with. He was as slippery as an eel. I'd run up against him in court a couple of times back when I was a cop; they were not pleasant encounters, at least for me. For him? I'd say they probably were.

"Harry Starke," he said, letting go of my hand, "take a seat. You, too, captain. To what do I owe this unexpected visit?" he asked heartily.

"To whom? Would be a more fitting question," I said as Kate and I sat down in the two inordinately expensive leather guest chairs. "Elizabeth Reynolds." I said and watched his expression change from jolly to shocked.

He bit his bottom lip, stared at me, then looked at Kate, then back at me.

"Elizabeth," he said finally. "After all these years. Why?"

"We don't think David Archer killed her," I said.

"But it was you that put him away," he replied, frowning. "What's changed?"

"New evidence," I said.

Still frowning, he asked, "What new evidence?"

I wasn't going to tell him, but Kate said, "Archer has an alibi, for one thing. And a confidential informant has been murdered."

Calling Amy Murphy a CI was a bit of a stretch, but I got her point.

"Where were you between the hours of five and seven on Wednesday evening, Mr. Stewart?" she asked.

"What?" he wrinkled his brow, eyes and nose. He sounded stunned.

"You heard me," she said. "Where were you between five and seven on Wednesday evening?"

"Surely you don't think…" he began, then paused, then swallowed, then glanced down at a large open day planner and continued, "I was here," he said. "From four when I got out of court, until after nine, working."

"Is there anyone who can corroborate that?" Kate asked.

He pressed a button on his desk phone and said, "Come in here for a moment, please, Angela."

The door opened, and an impeccably dressed young woman stepped inside. We'd already met her when we arrived, but I hadn't taken much notice of her, seated at her desk, as she was.

"This is my secretary, Angela Merchet," Stewart said. "Please tell these people where I was during the evening of Wednesday, October 26."

She frowned, looked taken aback. Then she looked at us through narrowed eyes and said, "What exactly is it you want to know?"

"We want to know," Kate began, her frustration clear, "where Mr. Stewart was between five and seven on Wednesday evening. It's simple enough and not yet two days ago."

She raised her head and looked down upon us, actually and figuratively. "He was here," she said haughtily, "working. That it?"

"You're sure?" Kate asked.

"Yes, I'm sure. Now. Are we done? I have a deposition to transcribe."

"You're sure he didn't leave, even for a few minutes," Kate pressed.

"Oh, for..." Stewart began. "What do you want? A written statement? That can be arranged."

Kate shook her head. "Calm down, Mr. Stewart. As a criminal defense attorney, you know how this goes. It's routine. We need to eliminate you from our inquiries... or not," she finished dryly.

"He was here," Angela said, quietly. "He didn't leave this office. I swear."

Well, that rules him out, I thought.

"Thank you, Angela," Kate said. "That's it. You may leave."

Angela looked at Stewart. He nodded, and she left.

"So, Harry," Kate said. "Do you have questions for Mr. Stewart?'

"I do," I said, "Where were you, Charlie, the night Elizabeth Reynolds was murdered? Friday July 12, 2001, between nine and eleven."

He stared at me. I could almost see the wheels turning inside his head.

He shook his head and said, “I have no earthly idea. It was twenty-one years ago. Do you know where you were that night? I bet you don’t. One thing I do know is I wasn’t with Elizabeth Reynolds.”

I smiled. He was right. I didn’t know where I was that night, so I let it go.

“She was an escort,” I said. “You were a client of hers?”

He thought for a moment, then nodded slowly. “I was,” he said, “but not the way you think.”

“She accompanied me to social events, functions, parties and so on. It was a professional relationship. Sex was never involved. Over the eighteen months or so we knew each other, we became friends. I was a young attorney trying to make a name for myself, and I needed a companion. It’s as simple as that. It was before I was married. My wife knows nothing about my relationship with Elizabeth, and I expect it to stay that way. Though, at the time, unlike most of the people who sought her company, I was not secretive about it. Back then, I didn’t care. Maybe I should have. You say Archer’s innocent. If he is, that means the killer is still out there. Maybe someone knows who it is and covered it up. Have you thought about that?”

I had, but his question made me wonder what he was thinking.

“Why do you say that?” I asked, frowning.

He looked at Kate, smiled grimly, then said, “We all know the answer to many crimes like this lies close to home.”

“Are you saying what I think you are?” Kate asked, frowning.

He shrugged. “You’re the detective, Captain, and, as such, I’m sure you’ve looked for motives. Who had the most to gain from her death if it wasn’t Archer?”

“You obviously think you know,” Kate replied, “so why don’t you tell me?”

“Actually, I don’t know,” he said, then paused, then continued, “I mentioned that Elizabeth and I became friends. While we were together, we talked a lot. I was curious about her lifestyle. She always smiled when I asked her about it, but she talked freely about it. No, she never mentioned any names, though I asked her many times. I also asked how she was able to operate with impunity from the law." Again, he paused and stared pointedly at Kate.

"And?" she said.

I smiled. I knew what was coming.

"She told me she had 'an arrangement.'" He made quotes with his fingers. "That she was paying someone off at the police department. No. She didn't tell me who it was. But suppose she was pressuring that someone. That, don't you think, would be motive enough to kill her?'

I pursed my lips. It was what I'd expected. And once again I thought about our three cops of interest, Miller, Finkle, and Whacker. I looked at Kate. She caught the look but ignored me.

"Why didn't you come forward?" she asked. "You didn't think to tell someone? That was important information."

"Oh, but I did," he said. "I told you I never made a secret of my relationship with Elizabeth. I was mortified when I heard what happened to her. I talked to Sergeant Miller. He took notes and said he'd look into it. I never heard from him again."

I frowned. It was news to me. It was my case. Miller was my immediate superior. He never mentioned interviewing Stewart to me.

"When did you talk to Miller?" I asked.

He shrugged. "I'm not exactly sure. Two, three days after her death."

I guess I need to talk to Miller again, I thought.

"Look," Stewart said. "I liked Elizabeth. She was my friend. I'm willing to help in any way that I can, short of involving my wife. But I told you everything I know and can remember. I have an appointment in…" He looked at his watch, then continued, "… ten minutes. Are we done?"

I looked at Kate and nodded.

"Very well, Mr. Stewart," she said, rising to her feet. "Thank you for your time and cooperation." She took a card from her jacket pocket and handed it across the desk to him.

He took it from her, looked at it, smiled, then said, "If I think of anything… Of course. I'll call you."

I also stood. "Thanks, Charlie," I said. "We appreciate your candor."

He stood, reached across the desk, and offered me his hand. "If there's anything I can do, Harry. Call me."

I shook his hand, and we left.

"That was a surprise," I said. "I expected him to be an ass, but that wasn't the Charlie Stewart I remember."

"Maybe he's mellowed over the years," Kate said. "The thing is, though, do you believe him?"

I made a face. "I think I do. How about you?"

I glanced at her. She shrugged, then nodded. "Yes, I do. We can cross him off our list. What about his conversation with Miller, though? Did you know about that?"

"No," I replied. "I think we should pay him a visit. You up for it?"

"It's just after eleven," she said. "Let's do it. I'd like to meet your old boss."

I glanced sideways at her. She was smiling.

22

It was twenty after eleven when we arrived at Tom Miller's home.

"Harry?" he said, frowning when he opened the front door.

"This is Captain Kate Gazzara, Tom," I said. "Can we come in? We need to talk."

Still frowning, he backed away, stood to one side, and waited until we were inside and the door was closed before he said, "What's this about, Harry? I told you everything I know." Then, almost as an afterthought, he looked at Kate and said, "Captain." He nodded to her in greeting, then said, "I was a little before your time, but I stay in touch. I've heard a lot about you. Please…" He waved a hand at the kitchen table. "Sit down. Both of you. Can I get you anything? Coffee, maybe?"

"Not for me, Tom, thanks," I said, taking a seat at the table.

"Captain?" he asked.

She shook her head. "No, thank you."

"Well, I need some," he said, "so give me a minute while I get it."

We watched as he poured a cup, his back turned toward us,

and I had to wonder if he wasn't playing for time as he wondered why we were there.

"So," he said as he sat down, smiling broadly, "what can I do for you? I already told you all I know."

"Not quite all, Tom," I said, quietly. "You omitted your interview with Charlie Stewart."

He stared at me for a moment, then laughed. "That was because there was nothing to tell," he said. He was still smiling, but now the smile was fixed, unnatural.

"Nothing to tell?" I said. "Are you shitting me, Tom? A noted defense attorney goes out of his way to tell you there are people in the department taking bribes from hookers and you didn't think it important? You never told me about it. Stewart said you took notes. How come you didn't give them to me?"

"He wasn't a prominent attorney then," he replied. "He was a lying piece of shit sleeping with one of the hookers. Who would have believed a word he said? Yeah, I tossed the notes. They weren't worth the paper they were written on."

"Wow," Kate said. "No wonder the wrong man was convicted."

"That was on him," Miller snapped, and pointed a shaking finger at me. "He put him away, not me. And who says he was the wrong man. No one's proved that to me yet."

This was a Tom Miller I'd never seen before, and I didn't like him.

"It was your duty to pass such information on to me, Tom," I said. "Who were you covering up for? Henry Finkle? Gordon Whacker?"

"I was covering up for no one, you arrogant..." He paused, obviously thinking better of what he'd been about to say, then continued, "No one. What d'you think I was, Harry? I was a good cop. Did I take advantage of... certain situations sometimes? Yeah, but didn't we all? But I never, not once, did I take a bribe. That I swear. Nor did I knowingly cover up for anyone who did."

"To answer your question, Tom," I said. "No, we didn't all take advantage of anyone. But you? You slept with the victim. Money or not, that's taking a bribe, and it's a felony. You could lose your pension."

Whether or not that was true, I wasn't sure. I figured it was, but it was something I didn't have to know.

"Why didn't you hand Stewart over to me?" I asked. "It would have opened up a whole new line of inquiry."

"And that's the point," he snapped. "The guy was lying. I tore that shit up the minute I saw the back of him."

"Well," I said. "You were wrong, and I think you know you were. Someone at the PD was taking bribes and that, as you well know, is motive. Had I had that information, things might have gone differently, and David Archer wouldn't have lost twenty-plus years of his life."

I paused for a moment, then looked at him and said, "Where were you that night, Tom, between nine and eleven?"

He stared at me open-mouthed, then snarled, "Screw you, Starke. It was twenty-one years ago. I don't remember. Where were you?"

I almost smiled. I didn't remember either.

"How about last Wednesday between five and seven?" I asked.

"What?" he said, frowning.

"Come on, Tom. It was just two days ago," I said.

He squinted at me, then said, "I was here."

"Can anyone corroborate that?" I asked.

He shook his head.

"You screwed up all those years ago, Tom," I said, rising to my feet. "I hope you can live with yourself. Come on, Kate. Let's get the hell out of here. It stinks."

And we did, and, as we walked back to the car in silence, I couldn't help but wonder what the man must be thinking. Knowing him as I did, I thought he was probably in denial.

"What d'you think, Kate?" I said as she climbed into the passenger seat.

"I think he's a lying sack of excrement," she replied. "And I think he destroyed his notes because he was covering for someone. Son of a bitch. Really?"

She shook her head. "Really?" she repeated.

"Come on, Kate," I said. "He isn't the first, nor will he be the last. You know that. What galls me, though, is the fact that he doesn't think there was anything wrong with what he did. The question for us, though, is—"

"Who was he covering up for?" she finished for me.

23

"You want to come back to the office with me and see what's going on, or do you want to go back to the PD?" I asked.

"The PD," she replied. "I need to go get Samson, and I need to talk to my team and see how their interviews went. Why? What's on your mind?"

"Are you working tomorrow?" I asked.

"Why? What are you thinking?" she asked.

"I'd like to talk to Soames. And then there's Whacker. What did you decide to do about him?"

"I still need to talk to the chief," she replied. "I'll do that when I get back this afternoon and let you know. No, tell you what. You come with me. That should be fun."

I glared at her. "Fun? Are you serious. Johnston hates my guts."

"No, he doesn't," she said. "He thinks highly of you, especially since you solved his daughter's murder. Besides," she added and grinned at me, "I like to see you squirm."

"Squirm my ass," I replied. "Okay. Let's do it."

She didn't reply. She just sat there gazing out through the windshield, smiling.

~

I never really got along with Chief Johnston. What we had when I was a detective sergeant was little more than an armed truce, but he respected me, though he didn't approve of my methods. He also respected the fact that I had a ninety-two percent closing rate. I was a good detective, and he knew it, which was why, even though I was no longer a cop, he came to me when his daughter Emily went missing. I solved it but, unfortunately, the ending wasn't a happy one. Since then, Kate roped me in as an unpaid consultant maybe a dozen times, always with Johnston's reluctant approval, as he had in this case.

So, it kinda made sense that Kate would want me there when she asked permission to interview an assistant chief, albeit a retired assistant chief. One, I figured it would be a tough sell and two, she didn't have the rank to interview him. That, I was sure, was why she wanted me along. Me? I didn't need the rank. What I did need was for Johnston to force the issue, or even preside over the event.

Kate knocked on the door of Chief Johnston's outer office, then opened the door and stepped inside.

Christy, Johnston's PA, was, as always, seated at her desk. She looked up and smiled as we entered.

"Harry Starke," she said. "Well, bless me. Long time no see. How are you, Harry?"

"I'm well," I said. "You? How's my nemesis?" I glanced at the chief's door.

She smiled. "As evil as he ever was. Me? I'm fine, thank you."

"Is he busy?" Kate asked.

"I'll see," she said and picked up the desk phone. "Captain Gazzara and Harry Starke are here to see you. You got it, Chief."

She hung up the phone and said, "He can give you fifteen minutes. You can go on in."

Kate nodded. I nodded. Kate stepped up to the door, knocked twice, opened it, and stepped inside. I followed, wondering why the hell I'd let her talk me into it.

Johnston, seated behind his desk, stood up as we entered.

"Well, well," he said as he rounded the desk and extended his hand to me. "The bad penny returns. How are you, Harry?"

"Oh, fair to middlin', I guess," I said, shaking his hand. His grip was firm, but not aggressively so.

"I want to thank you for agreeing to come in as a consultant on this Amy Murphy case," he said, returning to his seat. "Please, sit down. Any progress, Kate?"

"Some," she said, "which is why we're here, and why I insisted Harry accompany me. We've run up against a kinda tricky situation."

He frowned. It was an intimidating look he'd cultivated over the years. I remembered it well, and inwardly I smiled.

"Go on, Captain," he said, quietly.

The change from Kate to Captain was duly noted.

"What d'you know about Chief Whacker?" she asked.

For a moment, I could see he was quite taken aback, but he quickly recovered and said, "What's this about, Captain, and please be careful."

Never one to beat around the bush, Kate came right out with it. "I, that is we," she said and glanced at me, "think he's dirty."

Well, that was like hitting a screw with a sledgehammer when all that was needed was a screwdriver, and I swear I actually cringed. Kate, however, seemed totally unfazed as Johnston stared at her in amazement.

And he continued to stare at her for what seemed like minutes when, in fact, it was only a few seconds.

"You'd better be able to back that up, Captain," he said eventually.

"Well, you see, Chief," she said after clicking her tongue, "that's the problem. I can't. It's why we're here. We want to interview him."

At that, Johnston actually blanched. Me? By then, I was thoroughly enjoying myself.

"You what?" he asked, incredulously.

"We want to interview him," Kate insisted. "We've received credible information that indicates his activities past and present may have a direct bearing on both the Murphy and Elizabeth Reynolds cases."

Now that was a mouthful, and I couldn't help but admire her. She'd come a long way since she was my partner back in 2008, and I was proud of her.

"What information?" Johnston snapped.

Kate looked at me and nodded.

"Chief," I said. "We have information from a credible source that back in 2001, someone in the department was on the take. We also know for a fact that three police officers—two of them senior police officers—were clients of Elizabeth Reynolds, Whacker being one of them. The allegations that a senior police officer was taking bribes are reason enough to interview him. The allegations also provide a possible link to the murder of Amy Murphy."

Johnston opened his eyes wide, leaned back in his chair and folded his arms. He thought for a moment, then said, "And this credible source is?"

"In the interest of protecting the source," Kate said, "we think it's best if we keep the name confidential, at least for the time being."

"And you want me to order an interrogation of a senior police officer on what?" he growled. "The word of an unidentified individual who may or may not be lying. Not to mention you don't have the rank."

"First," Kate said, "the individual has an impeccable reputation and is not given to lying. Second, I don't intend to conduct the interrogation, as you call it. Harry will do that. He doesn't need the rank. He would like your agreement, of course, but he doesn't need it. He, as you know from personal experience, is an excellent… interrogator."

I had to smile at that one. "Chief," I said. "She's right. I don't need your permission, but don't you think it would be better, even easier, if we had your approval? And I'd like Kate to sit in. She can't do that without it."

He thought for a moment and was about to speak when I beat him to it.

"There is an alternative," I said. "You could sit in, too, preside over the proceedings, if you will."

There followed a long period of silence. And then, finally, he said, "Very well. I'll arrange it. Nine o'clock Monday morning. This office. That's all. You may go now. And Kate, keep this to yourself."

"Of course," she replied. And with that, we left his office, both a little out of breath, and both a little excited. I didn't know about Kate, but it was a first for me.

"So, what d'you think?" she asked as we walked out into the parking lot.

I shook my head. "From what I remember of Whacker— which isn't much— the man was almost a ghost. —He's a shrewd, arrogant son of a…" I trailed off. Then I had a thought.

"Hey, how about that rape kit?"

"Oh yeah, that," she replied. "I sent it over to the lab. Nothing yet. It takes a while. You know that."

I nodded. "And the Tiffany engagement ring?"

"Now that..." she said. "No. It's not in the evidence box."

"What?" I said, frowning. "It has to be. I bagged and tagged it myself."

"Sorry," she replied. "I looked. I promise. It's not there."

"Geez," I said. "Then what the hell happened to it?"

"I guess someone snagged it," she said. "Was it valuable?"

"Tiffany?" I said. "You bet it was. I had it valued before I booked it in. Just a rough estimate. But it was worth at least fifteen grand back then. Heaven only knows what it would be worth today."

"Well, I'll have IA look into it. I hate having to deal with them, but if somebody stole it, we have a problem. Not to mention the loss of the evidence. I gotta go get Samson. I'll talk to you in the morning."

"Yeah, you do that," I replied, wondering what the hell had happened to the ring. "Have a good one, Kate. Tell Tom hello for me."

"Don't call him that," she said, smiling as she opened her car door. "He likes to be called Thomas."

"Oh yeah," I said, dryly. "Of course he does."

Then Kate headed home to get Samson, and I went back to my office.

24

IT WAS JUST AFTER TWO-THIRTY WHEN I WALKED INTO THE OUTER office to be greeted by Lucy, who told me Jacque needed to see me.

"Hey," I said, as I poked my head into Jacque's office. "What's up?"

"Come in and shut the door," she said.

"That sounds ominous," I replied. "Has something happened?"

"It has," she said, smiling. "Were you serious when you said you wanted to hire another investigator?"

I frowned. "Yes, but… why the air of mystery?"

"I had a call, about an hour ago…" She paused, smiling at me.

"Well… Go on."

"From Bob Ryan."

I stared at her, openmouthed. "No…" I said.

She nodded.

"Oh, for Pete's sake, Jacque. What did he want?"

"He's retired from the CIA. He wants to know if he can come back."

I didn't know what to say. Bob Ryan was one of the best

friends I ever had. I hired him back in 2008 when I first opened my agency, right after I hired Jacque and Tim. I was thirty-six. Bob was thirty-seven. His resume said he was a Marine and an ex-Chicago PD cop, and I had no reason to doubt it. As it turned out, he was CIA, and the resume was a concoction. What drew me to their attention, I never found out. I made him and Jacque partners in my company, and then, after nearly ten years, he just up and left. No word of explanation. He just… left. I found out later he'd been recalled and was station chief in a remote province of Afghanistan. I heard nothing more from him until November 2019 when I was being transported to Texas to face trial on a bogus charge of murdering a Texas Ranger. Then he appeared out of nowhere and broke me out of the transport vehicle. What happened next was an unlikely adventure together in Mexico, but that's another story. Suffice it to say, when he knew I was safe and in the clear, he disappeared again, and I've heard nothing from him since. If I was a cat, I would owe him three of my nine lives.

And now this.

"What did he have to say?" I asked after a moment of thought.

"Not much," she replied, "just that he'd taken early retirement, was on the loose, and looking for something to do."

"Wow," I said, lost for words. The prospect of Bob's return was a little overwhelming.

"What are you 'tinkin', Harry?" she said, sharply. "If you're serious about hiring someone, you should be rushin' out to meet him. Here, that's his number." She handed me a slip of paper.

I took it from her, stared at it for a moment, thinking. Then I took out my phone, punched in the number and waited. He answered on the second ring.

"Bob Ryan."

"When can you start?" I asked.

Jacque grinned up at me.

"Harry?" he said. "Damn! Is that you?"

"Yeah, it's me, you piece of shit. What the hell took you so long?"

I sat down… No; I dropped into the seat in front of Jacque's desk.

"And hello to you, too," he replied. "Geez, Harry. How the hell are you?'

What followed was one of those conversations you make once or twice in a lifetime, and it was one I don't want to even try to relay. Bob was, to me, the brother I never had.

Suffice it to say, the conversation ended on a high note with his return scheduled for Monday, the 14th of November.

I hung up, stared at the phone for a moment, smiling to myself. Then I looked at Jacque and said, "All we need now is for Ronnie Hall to come back and the gang will be all here."

She stood up, came around her desk, threw her arms around my neck, and hugged me.

"I'm so excited," she said, letting go of me. "I can't wait."

"Yeah, well. Me too, but we have work to do. Let's leave the celebrating until he gets here."

"Can I tell Tim?" she asked.

I nodded, and she almost ran from the room. Me? I went upstairs to my office and was about to sit down when Tim came rushing in.

"Harry!" he yelled. "I can't believe it. I wanna hear it from you. He's coming back, right? Bob?"

"So he said," I replied, quietly.

"Wow! Wow, wow, wow. That's great. That's—"

"Calm down, Tim," I said.

He stood there staring at me, grinning and biting his top lip at the same time. He looked… I want to say insane, but he's far from that. Tim is, in many ways, just a kid. Bob, as you can imagine, was very special to him. Especially because Tim didn't have a father in his life, or a brother.

"Go get the others, Tim." I said. "We need to wrap things up and get out of here."

Tim was back five minutes later, followed by TJ, then a couple of minutes later by Jacque and finally Heather.

"I'm sure Tim has given you the good news," I said, "so let's say no more about it. It's early days yet. And, talking about early days, I'd like one. Heather?"

She looked at TJ, then said, "Walter Jeffries, the accountant, is in Europe. England, to be precise, and has been since October 4, visiting his wife's family. I called him. He sounded open enough. He admitted he'd seen Reynolds maybe four times, though he wasn't even sure about that. He can't remember where he was the night she was killed."

"Could he have returned, d'you think, and killed Murphy?" I asked.

She shrugged. "Anything's possible, I suppose." She looked at Tim, her eyebrows raised.

"Sure," he said. "I'll check the flights from London."

"Simian Woodley," Heather said. "I find it hard to believe he could have killed Murphy. He's in his eighties and walks with a cane and gets around on one of those mobility scooters, or whatever they're called. He's also divorced, over thirty years, and freely admits he was one of Reynold's regular customers, and he came across as proud of it. Said she was a lovely girl with a lovely temperament—his words, not mine. But he, too, cannot remember where he was the night she was killed. He's an affable old man," she said. "I liked him."

She looked at TJ. He smiled at her.

"I don't think he was lying" she said, "and he doesn't have it in him, physically, to have killed Murphy. Nor do I think he has the ability."

I nodded. "Do either of you think we need to talk to them further?"

Heather looked at TJ. He nodded, once.

"Not at this time," she said. "I think we can take them off the list."

"So what now?" TJ asked.

"Kate and I, mostly Kate," I said, "talked to Johnston. She was able to persuade him to let us interview Gordon Whacker in his office on Monday. In the meantime, I'm waiting on a report from Kate's team as to how their interviews went. Other than the Soames interview I'm supposed to do tomorrow, there's little more we can do."

"That it for today, then?" Jacque asked.

"That's it," I said, and thanked everyone for their efforts, then said, "Go home. Have a good weekend. I'll see y'all on Monday."

25

I SPENT THE NEXT HALF-HOUR TALKING TO JACQUE, PARTIALLY about the case, but mostly about Bob Ryan's return.

Me? I was still a little skeptical that it would happen, and even a little apprehensive that it would.

We'd been close, Bob and I. He'd saved my tail more times than I could count. He killed, when necessary, without hesitation or regret. But then, on thinking about it, so did I. Isn't it funny how you can't see in yourself what you see in others?

We talked about Mexico, as we often did. They were all there, my team and family, even Tim. And then Bob turned up out of the blue. How he knew I was in trouble, I don't know. He never said, and I never asked him. I always assumed it was through his CIA connections. And that brought up another question: "Why was he assigned to spy on me, Jacque?" I asked.

"You don't know?" she replied.

I shook my head. "No, I don't know."

"Think about it, Harry? Who were you involved with at the time?"

I frowned. "You're talking about Congressman Harper?"

"No, Harry. Think again."

I narrowed my eyes. "You're not talking about Linda. Senator Linda Michaels?"

"I am," Jacque replied.

"But why would the CIA be interested in her?" I asked. "She was chairman of the Senate Appropriations Committee, so the FBI I could understand, but not the CIA."

"She was also chairman of the Senate Foreign Affairs Committee," Jacque said. "That made her a very important member of the senate, second only to the Leader."

"I didn't know that," I said, frowning. "How did you know that?"

"It's my job to know what and who you're doing," she said with a sly smile on her face. "Whatever happened to the lovely senator from Boston, by the way?"

"I met Amanda, is what happened," I replied.

"D'you ever hear from her, the senator?" she asked.

"Once in a while, yes."

"And?" Jacque asked, smiling.

"And I hear from her. Nothing untoward. Just friendly contact. That's all."

"That was a pretty intense affair you had with her, wasn't it?"

I thought about it for a moment. The conversation was becoming a little uncomfortable for me.

"It wasn't an affair," I said. "Neither of us was married. She was, as you said, an important politician, way above my paygrade. And she had… problems. Let's leave it at that."

She nodded, then said, "Back to Bob. Are you going to reinstate him as a partner?"

I'd thought about that in some depth. I'd thought so much of Bob I'd given him twenty-five percent of my company. I'd revoked it after he left. Now what?

I shook my head. "No, Jacque. That's not going to happen. Now, if that's it…" I looked at my watch. "I need to go home. I'm supposed to meet with Kate in the morning. We planned to go talk to the Soames woman, but I'm thinking I might put it off until next week."

"Then you should go, Harry," she replied. "I'll see you Monday morning, then?"

"Yep. Not sure what time. My appointment with Johnston is at nine."

"Whenever, Harry. Have a good weekend."

IT WAS JUST after six-thirty when I left the office that evening. It had been a dull day, overcast, and it was already dark. That being so, I couldn't help but catch the headlights in my rearview mirror that followed me the length of Broad Street to Cummings Highway. I became certain I was being followed when the vehicle stayed with me as I took the split to Scenic Highway.

I drove on for about a mile, then turned into the Ruby Falls parking lot and stopped the car. Sure enough, the lights followed just a few seconds later and the same black SUV pulled up alongside me.

I drew my weapon and stepped out of the car, my gun pointed at the driver's side window, which was kind of stupid, seeing as I couldn't see through the tinted glass.

The side window rolled down to reveal... Geez, I thought. What the hell?

Tom Miller had both hands in the air. "I just wanna talk, Harry," he said.

"Get out of the car, Tom," I replied, holstering the CZ.

"What do you want, Tom? And why couldn't you have just called me instead of following me around? That sort of thing can get you killed."

"Yeah, kinda stupid, right?" he replied. "I wanted to talk to you, on the QT. Off the record, like. If… If they find out I talked to you… It was Amy, Harry. I knew her. For years, I knew her. She was a nice kid. She didn't deserve to die like that."

"What do you know about it, Tom?" I asked.

"Nothing," he said. "Not about her death, but that's why you asked me where I was this morning, right? You knew she was dead. What happened, Harry? She talk to you? People still die around you, don't they, Harry?"

"You got something to say to me, Tom, say it."

"This is off the record, Harry. No one can know I talked to you. And I won't testify. Got it?"

I nodded.

"And you promise you won't mention my name?"

"I won't," I said. "Now spit it out."

"Harry, there are powerful people in play here. People with secrets. Secrets they will do anything to keep."

"Who are these powerful people?" I asked.

"I don't have no names, Harry, except for Henry Finkle, but he knows. Look, it ain't just him. I was just the low man on the totem pole. I had to do what I was told. If I didn't… Harry, I was never a dirty cop, but I had to play the game. I covered some shit up I shouldn't have. See, Finkle caught me with Elizabeth. He has photos. Of me and her. I mean they're graphic, Harry. How the hell he got 'em, I never found out, but he gave me copies and… well, you can guess the rest."

"Blackmail?" I asked.

He nodded. "I would have lost my career, my pension, everything. Last Wednesday, after you left, I got a call. I don't know who it was; the voice was muffled. They said if I talked to you again, I'd regret it. Well, I got scared, and I followed you. I was going to stop when you pulled over on the mountain, but I lost my nerve. Then you come around this morning and, man, I got to thinking. So here I am, and you'd better not say anything."

"This is all well and good, Tom," I said. "But I need names."

He shook his head. "Except for Finkle, I don't have any. There was one guy, though. I don't know what his connection was. He called me several times, wanted to talk, said he had information, but Finkle wouldn't let me follow up. He said he knew the guy and would deal with it himself. I never heard from him again. His name was Brendan Loftin. That's all I know."

I made a note of the name, then said, "And you didn't bother to run the guy's sheet?"

"Yeah, I did. He was clean. There was nothing on him."

"What did he want?" I asked. "Did he tell you anything at all?"

Miller shook his head. "No, he just said it was important."

"And you didn't bother to follow it up?" I said. "Geez. Why didn't you pass it on to me?"

"Hah, Finkle told me to forget it. So I did. And anyway, you was a damn hothead back then. Harry, you need to be very careful uncovering these old secrets. They already killed Amy. They won't stop. And be especially careful around Finkle. He's dirty, but he ain't the guy in charge. Take it from me."

"What d'you know about Gordon Whacker?" I asked him.

He swallowed, then looked at me and said, "I don't know, Harry. Honestly. I don't. There were rumors, and Finkle was always up his ass, but Finkle was always up somebody's ass. Still is, from what I hear. But Whacker?" He shook his head. "I don't know. He retired a few years ago, so I heard. That's it, Harry. We're done. Don't contact me again, okay?"

He turned and got back into his car and drove away.

I watched him go. Had I learned anything? Sure. I'd learned I needed to be very careful from that point on.

26

My conversation, if you can call it that, with Tom Miller didn't last but a few minutes. As I watched him turn out of the Ruby Falls parking lot onto Scenic Highway and head down the mountain, I couldn't help but wonder if all he'd said was true.

It was seven-thirty when I arrived home that evening. Jade was still up and full of energy, though I could tell it was beginning to wane. Even so, as I sat at the kitchen table, she crawled under the table and then up onto my lap and demanded I tell her a story.

"Only if you go to bed like a good little girl," I said in my best impression of Little Red Riding Hood's wolf. She giggled and wriggled down onto the floor and ran to get her story book. I put her to bed ten minutes later without a peep of protest.

"She wants you to kiss her goodnight," I said to Amanda when I came downstairs. And she did, to return a few minutes later looking… Okay, I'm going to say it: delicious.

"How was your day?" she asked as she placed a plate of steaming hot beef stew in front of me, and then a glass of Cabernet. "Go ahead," she said. "Don't wait for me."

The stew was amazing, the wine—though not expensive—

excellent, and the company? Well, I don't have to comment on that, now do I?

"So, how was your day?" she repeated as she sat down and took a sip of her wine.

"Interesting is the word, I suppose," I replied.

"Do tell," she said, and took a sip of her wine.

So I did. I told her about our morning visit to Steward and the subsequent Miller revisit, and our interview with Johnston. And finally, I told her about Miller chasing me down on my way home. All this while I was eating my stew.

I finished my dissertation and my dinner, and I settled back in my chair and looked at her, my eyebrows raised in question.

"That was quite a day," she said, "and I do hope you're taking Miller's warning seriously. Your perp, as you like to call them, has killed again, and that doesn't bode well, Harry."

I shrugged, but didn't answer.

"Not the reaction I was hoping for," she said dryly and took a sip of her wine. "So, what's your plan? You obviously have one."

"Actually, I don't," I replied. "Other than a quiet weekend. I had planned to talk to the Soames woman with Kate tomorrow morning, but I think I'll give it a pass and talk to her on Monday after we're done with Whacker and the chief."

"Oh goody," she said, again dryly. "We'll have you all to ourselves… Seriously, though, what are you going to do about Henry?"

I hadn't thought about that… Well, I had, but only in passing. But Amanda was right. I had to do something—the guy was dirty—but what?

"I don't know," I said, after a brief moment of thought and a sip of wine. "Turn him in to IA, I suppose. If I do it, it will save Kate the embarrassment of having to do it. Or maybe I'll turn it over to the chief and let him deal with it."

She nodded. "That would probably be the best way to do it.

Right now, you need something to take your mind off it. How about we watch a show? I'd like to watch Pride and Prejudice."

"You go ahead," I said. "I need a moment or two to think. What's it like outside, I wonder?"

"Oh, Harry," she said. "You really are incorrigible."

I grinned at her and said, "My mother used to tell me that. I won't be long."

And I wasn't. I walked out onto the patio, drink in hand, but since I'd arrived home, the weather had set in and the mountaintop was covered in a blanket of white clouds. Now you might be thinking of fluffy white clouds like cotton candy. Not so. It was dank, wet, and the visibility was down to less than twenty feet.

Not to be deterred, though, I went to the covered area and sat down at one of the concrete tables.

So who? I thought. *It's someone we know, or should know. I'm sure of it. Henry Finkle? Hmm, he's at the heart of the conspiracy, for that's what it is, a conspiracy to cover up the murder of Elizabeth Reynolds. But just how deep does the conspiracy go? Henry's deeply involved, but I'm fairly sure he's not the head of the snake. That's someone higher up. How much higher? That's another question, isn't it? Whacker? He seems the most likely suspect, but we have yet to talk to him. Oh hell—*

It was beginning to rain, and a strong breeze was blowing across the mountain. There wasn't a dry spot outside the house. So I grabbed my glass and made a run for it.

"That show begun yet?" I asked Amanda. She was in the kitchen cleaning up.

"No. It's on Prime. That didn't take long," she said without turning round. "What happened?"

"It's raining," I said, "and blowing up a storm, I think. Quit what you're doing and let's go settle down for an hour or two."

She turned, put her hands on her hips and gave me one of those looks.

"Yes, m'lord," she said and did the prettiest curtsy.

"I didn't know you knew how to do that," I said.

"There's a lot you don't know about me, Harry Starke," she said. "So go pour yourself a glass of scotch and let's do it."

And we did.

27

The weekend went by quickly. Saturday was a quiet relaxing day spent doing chores around the outside of the house. On Sunday I played golf with my father, had lunch at the club, and then I spent the afternoon at home reading, something I'm rarely able to find the time for these days. All in all, it was a pleasant respite from the rigors of running a business, albeit a small one.

So, it was with no little anticipation when I set out for the police department that Monday morning.

I'd purposely not contacted anyone from the office during those two days, so, as I drove down the mountain, I called Tim and asked him to run a background check on Brendan Loftin. Then I called Jacque and let her know where I was and that I'd be in later. That done, I drove to the PD with a clear head.

I parked out front and walked inside to find Kate and Samson waiting for me in the lobby. It was eight-fifty-five.

Kate was dressed in jeans, a blue shirt, and an off-white leather jacket. Samson was wearing his harness and badge. They made quite a team.

"Good morning," she said as I checked in. "They're waiting for us."

"As I expected," I said as I reached down to scratch behind Samson's ears. "How you doing, boy?"

He rewarded me with a toothy grin that told me all I wanted to know.

"Is he here?" I asked as we walked down the corridor to Johnston's offices.

"Yes, and he's not happy," she replied. "I know I told him you'd do the interview, but I think you'd better let me do the talking." She glanced at me and said, "And you be careful what you say. He has a… Just be careful, that's all."

I was happy to go along with that, to an extent. I never had much contact with Whacker. He was the Vice commander, and I was Homicide, but I was familiar with his reputation and his type. They were rebels, spent most of their time out of uniform, as did we, but Vice is different. They have to blend in. Make dubious friendships. Thus, they become… I don't know. Outsiders is not quite the word, but you get the idea. Whacker came up through the ranks with the street engrained in his DNA.

Christy was at her desk. She nodded to Kate as we entered the chief's outer office and then at the closed door to the inner sanctum.

"What kind of mood is he in?" Kate asked.

"Quiet," Christy replied, "so be careful. He's at his most dangerous when he's quiet."

I shook my head. *Geez,* I thought. *Am I ever glad I'm out of this mess?*

Kate stepped up to the door, knocked once, and opened it. I winked at Christy, and she smiled up at me and said, "Harry."

I followed Kate into the room, determined to hold my own, no matter what. I didn't fall under the confines of police department protocols and etiquette and could, so I thought, conduct myself accordingly.

Gordon Whacker was seated in front and to the left of the chief's desk. He stood when we entered and turned to face Kate.

He was tall, slim, with white hair and a mustache, heavy brows and a sharp nose. He was dressed in blue jeans, a white shirt open at the neck, and a blue suit jacket, almost a twin to what I was wearing.

"What the hell is this about, Captain?" he began, his anger front and center. "Why have I been dragged in here at this ungodly hour on a Monday morning?" He looked down at Samson and said, "And why the dog? What do you think I am? Some sort of low life criminal?" He then turned his attention to me. "Starke! What are you doing here?"

"Good morning, Mr. Whacker," Kate said, extending her hand and smiling at him. "Samson accompanies me wherever I go. Thank you for coming. We have a few questions, if you don't mind—"

"I do mind," he snapped, cutting her off. "What questions? How long is this going to take? I have an urgent appointment at—"

"Then why don't we get on with it?" Kate said. "Shall we sit down?"

The chief sat upright in his chair, his arms folded across his chest, maintaining an air of silent authority. Kate sat down in the center chair while I took the one to the right. Samson lay down at Kate's feet, his tongue lolling, panting gently.

"Mr. Starke is here as a consultant," Kate said. "I take it you know him."

He glanced at me and looked quickly away, and I wondered why.

"Yes, I know him," he said, "by reputation only. Our paths

never crossed. Oh, do get on with it, Captain," he finished irritably.

"What is your relationship with Lana Baudette?" she asked.

The question didn't faze him one bit.

"She's a friend," he said. "A long-time friend. I met her through the job. Why do you ask?"

"When did you meet her?" Kate asked.

"Hmm. I'm not sure. Ninety-nine, 2000, perhaps. It was a long time ago. And I'll ask you again, why do you ask?"

"Bear with me, Mr. Whacker. I'll get there," Kate replied. "You know, of course, that she's in the sex for hire business?"

"I wouldn't call it that, but yes, she runs an escort service, or she did. What she's up to these days, I have no idea."

"Knowing that she was pimping prostitutes, did you or your team ever arrest her?"

"No. I… There was never any evidence… What the hell are you getting at, Captain? Are you accusing me of something?"

"Of course not, Mr. Whacker," she replied sweetly. "I'm simply trying to establish a baseline. You were saying?"

"There was never any evidence that she was in the business of prostitution."

"Did you ever avail yourself of her services—"

"What the hell?" He jumped to his feet. So did Samson.

"Chief Johnston," he snapped, "are you going to allow her to talk to me like this? She's trying to besmirch my reputation."

"Sit down, Gordon," Johnston said. "Nothing said in this room will leave it. Just answer the questions and we can all get on with whatever it was we were doing." He looked at Kate and said, "Be careful, Captain."

"Of course, Chief," she replied, gifting him with a wide smile. "Aren't I always?"

He gave her a wry look at that, but didn't reply. Whacker sat down again. So did Samson. I looked down at the big dog and smiled to myself. He glanced round at me and damn if he didn't seem to nod at me.

"So," Kate said, brightly. "Where were we? Oh yes…" She locked eyes with him and said, "Did you ever avail yourself of Lana Baudette's services?"

"No, damn it. I didn't," he snapped.

"We have a witness that will testify that you did," Kate lied.

"Then that witness is a damn liar," he snapped.

"How well did you know Elizabeth Reynolds?" Kate asked.

"Who?" he asked, frowning.

"Elizabeth Reynolds," Kate said. "She worked for Lana Baudette in 2000 and 2001."

"I'm not familiar with the name," he said and looked away to his left. I smiled. He caught it.

"Reynolds, you say?" he said, his brow furrowed. "You don't mean…? Are you talking about the girl who was murdered? Oh yes, I remember. Didn't you put her killer away for life, Starke?"

There was a lot I could have said in answer to that, but I chose to remain silent. So I nodded instead.

"No, I didn't know her at all," he said to Kate.

"Would it surprise you then," Kate said, "that my witness says you did know her, and that you knew her very well?"

"As I said, your witness is a damn liar," he replied. "Who is this witness?"

"But you did know her?" Kate insisted, ignoring his question.

"In passing, yes. So technically, I suppose I did know her, but that's all," he replied.

"Where were you on the night of July 12, 2001, between the hours of nine and eleven?" Kate asked.

"Oh, for God's sake," he said and looked at the chief and said, "Wesley?"

"Answer the question, Gordon," Johnston said, stoically.

"I don't know, do I?" he replied, sounding exasperated. "It

was twenty-one years ago. How could I possibly be expected to remember anything that far back?"

"Let's bring it forward twenty-one years, then," Kate said. "Where were you between the hours of five and seven last Wednesday evening?"

"What?" He frowned. "Why d'you want to know?"

"Just answer the question, please, Mr. Whacker," Kate replied.

"I was at home. All evening. You can ask my wife."

"We will," Kate said. "And what were you doing while you were at home all evening?"

"Relaxing, mostly, watching television. Look, what's this about? Is it about Amy Murphy?"

"You know about her?" Kate asked.

"Of course," he replied. "It's been on TV all weekend."

"How well did you know her?" Kate asked.

"I didn't say I knew her," he replied, smiling.

"But you did, didn't you?" Kate asked.

He nodded. "Yes, I knew Amy, poor girl. She was one of Lana's escorts. She's been out of the business for a long time. She was one of my detective's CIs, but that ended when she quit. She had a big drug problem, as I recall. I last saw her a couple of weeks ago. In the diner where she works… worked. I was sorry to hear about what happened to her. A drug overdose, according to the TV… Unless…? Oh, I see. You think she was murdered. That's why you want to know where I was. Well, as I said, I was home all night."

"Did you ever take hush money from Lana Baudette?" Kate asked.

He glanced at Johnston, then at me, then back at Kate, and smiled. "No, Captain, I did not. Now, if we're done, I need to be on my way." He stood up, inclined his head at Kate, nodded at me, then walked confidently to the door and left.

Kate rubbed her eyes, looked at me, then at Johnston and said, "That went well, not!"

She looked at me and said, "What do you think, Harry?"

"He lied about knowing Reynolds, but then caught on and rectified it. Other than that..." I shrugged. "It's hard to say. I wouldn't trust him as far as I could throw him, but it was hard to find fault with his answers. Was he using Lana's hookers? Did he know Reynolds? I don't know. How well did he know Murphy? I don't know that either, and there's not much use checking his alibi. His wife will, no doubt, back him to the hilt. You might be able to tell if she's lying, though, and if she is, that would open up a new line of inquiry. What do you think, Chief?"

"Much as you do, Harry," he replied, then looked at Kate and said, "Let it go for now, Kate. I know him. He's a vindictive son of a bitch and hounding him will only antagonize him."

"He certainly gave little away," Kate said. "I will have someone check his alibi, though."

"Chief, I have a question, but you're not going to like it." I said.

"Go ahead, Harry. I trust your judgment. If I didn't, you wouldn't be here."

"Do you know that Henry Finkle is dirty?" I asked.

I heard Kate's sharp intake of breath.

I watched Johnston's expression turn from benign to hard. His eyes narrowed and his mouth opened slightly, and he stared at me.

"You'd better have some damn good evidence to back that allegation up," he said.

I looked at Kate. She looked back at me as if to say, you're on your own here, buddy.

"We have several witnesses that—"

"Stop," he raised a hand, cutting me off. "Are these witnesses prepared to testify in court?"

I thought about Miller, Baudette, Stewart. I looked again at Kate. She slowly shook her head.

"I guess not," I said, reluctantly.

"I thought not," Johnston said. "Now let me tell *you* something. And it's not to leave this room. Understood?"

We both nodded.

"You asked if I knew he was dirty," he continued. "The answer is yes. I've known for years. Unfortunately, proving it is another story. I demoted him for what he did to Kate. It was little enough, I know, but he's a wily one, is our Henry, and until I can get something solid on him, there's nothing I can do. But, I will also say this: his time will come. Now, if there's nothing else, I have work to do."

"Thank you, Chief," I said, rising to my feet.

And we made to leave.

"Kate," he said, as she put her hand on the door handle. "Keep him in line."

I turned, grinned at him, and said, "When could she ever, Chief, or even you, for that matter?"

"Get out of here, Starke, before I lock you up," he said, smiling.

28

"IT'S A BIT EARLY," I SAID, AS WE STOOD TOGETHER ON THE front porch of the police department. "What would you like to do? Lunch or Soames?"

She looked at her watch, then said, "You're right. It's barely eleven. Soames lives just across the river. Let's see what she has to say for herself. You bring the images?"

"I did. Let's do it."

And it was a glorious day for it. The cloudless sky was the palest blue, the river almost a sheet of glass. I drove across the CB Robinson Bridge to the North Access, and from there to Hixson Pike and from there to Carter Drive and the Enclave, Charlie Maxwell's old hunting ground.

Who was Charlie Maxwell, you ask? Ah, Charlie. She, or should I say he, was one of my past loves, or would have been, had I not found she was a trans. Unfortunately, she was murdered to shut her up. That was back in 2015. I hadn't yet met Amanda; and Kate… well, she… I looked at her and smiled. She had no idea what I was thinking, and it was better that she shouldn't. But back to Charlie. She was a beautiful woman, too darned beautiful. She died trying to pass information to me that would have put

Congressman Gordon "Little Billy" Harper away for life, which it did once I'd figured it out. But that's another life and another story. We're here to talk about the David Archer case.

Janice Soames lived in a half-million-dollar, two-story house on the banks of the Tennessee River in the upscale Enclave community, and she was home.

She came to the door dressed in what I think should be called a kaftan, a diaphanous affair that, voluminous as it was, left no detail undiscovered, especially as the light shone through it as we followed her to the living room.

Kate had already introduced us both, and she seemed unfazed by Samson's presence, nor him with her, which was a good sign. Kate, and by association, me, had learned a while ago to trust his almost supernatural instincts.

She was tall, almost as tall as Kate, poised. She was, by any definition, a beautiful woman. It was an ageless beauty. Skin unblemished and wrinkle free, hazel eyes sparkling, hair dyed a subtle shade of… almost silver. I knew her to be forty-four years old, but she didn't look a day over twenty-five.

"So, Captain, Harry, what can I do for you?' she asked as she spun around, her back to the floor-to-ceiling window. The silhouette was intoxicating. "But please, do sit down. Can I get you something to drink? Lemonade, perhaps? I make it myself. It's very refreshing."

Was it all an act? I wondered as we sat down together on the white leather couch. Something she'd developed over the many years of… entertaining? I was sure that it was. But if it was, it was beautifully done.

"We're here to talk to you about this," Kate said, laying out one of the website images on the coffee table in front of her.

"Oh, that's me,' she said, leaning forward to get a closer look. The already too low neck of the Kaftan opened like a flower and gifted me with a view almost all the way down to her toes. I hastily looked away, wondering if I'd already damaged my eyes.

"Why, that was very gentlemanly of you, Harry," she said, grasping the flimsy material and covering herself up. "Thank you."

"Don't mention it," I muttered.

"Really?" Kate asked sarcastically. "Can we get on with it, please?"

"Of course," she replied. "Are you sure you wouldn't like some lemonade? It really is good."

We both declined and Kate said, "You've been in the business a long time?"

"Yes, I have. Don't you think Starlight is a lovely name?" She looked at me as she said it and winked, a very subtle, practiced wink.

"It is," I said. "Have you always worked for Lana Baudette?"

"Oh, but I don't work for her, darling. I'm what you call an independent contractor. Isn't that funny? One would think I was a brick mason or something." And she laughed, then said, "But yes, Lana has always looked after my affairs."

"And, so I understand," I said, "you were a friend of Elizabeth Reynolds."

"Oh, yes. Liz and I were the best of friends," she replied. "I was stricken when she was… murdered…"

She got it, I thought

"Wait a minute," she said. "Aren't you… Yes… Yes, you are. I thought the name was familiar. You're that police officer that put her killer away. You're Harry Starke. Why are you here?"

Her voice had hardened, and suddenly she looked her age.

"We, that is I, think we convicted the wrong man. We've reopened the investigation, and we think you might be able to help."

"Are you serious?" she asked. "After all this time? How am I supposed to help?"

"You were her friend," I said. "You knew her friends, her contacts, her clients."

"Well, yes, some of them, but," she said and shrugged, "I still don't know how I can help."

"Can you think of anyone who might have wanted to harm her?" I asked.

She slowly shook her head. "No-oo… Not that I can think of. You know, I always wondered if that boy really did it. They were such good friends, since they were children, so I heard."

"Was she frightened of anyone?" I persisted.

"No-oo… I don't think so… Hmm, hmm. There was this one guy. She wasn't too happy with him. A client. Not one of Lana's. One she freelanced. She said he liked to… You know. He had trouble… Oh, you know what I'm talking about. He had trouble getting it up. He almost strangled her to death. She called me. The marks on her neck. It was outrageous. She said she never wanted to see him again after that, but he kept calling her, insisting she see him, but she wouldn't."

"Did she tell you his name?" I asked.

She shook her head. "No. I'm not sure she knew it herself. She said he was worried that his dealings with her would get out, and if they did, his reputation would be ruined. I told her to call the police, but of course she wouldn't."

"When was the last time she saw him, do you know?" I asked.

"Hmm, a week? Maybe two," she replied.

"And you know nothing about him?" I pressed her.

She shook her head. "She was very secretive about her private clients," she replied. "She said they trusted her and that was a good thing. Me? I let Lana handle things. She's always treated me well. Why wouldn't I?"

"You've been in the business a long time," Kate said. "How do you do that?" Kate looked at her, obviously puzzled.

Again, she nodded. "As I said, Lana looks after me. The money's good. I have enough set aside that I can retire whenever I want and never have to work again."

"But—" Kate began. But she cut her off.

"I know what you're going to say," she said. "Sex with so many different men. Captain, first of all, I'm very picky. Second, I'm an escort in the true sense of the word. Rarely do I have sex with my clients. And when…" She paused, looked at Kate through narrowed eyes and said, "All this is off the record, right?"

"I'm Homicide," Kate said, "not Vice. You can talk freely."

Soames nodded, then said, "As I was saying, when I do have sex with a client, it's always my choice. Liz, however, was all about the money. She was desperate to get out of the business. Thus her choices were sometimes… questionable. And look where it got her." She looked at me and continued, "I never thought David killed her, and I would have said so had I been asked. I think she died at the hands of a client."

"Why didn't you come forward at the time?" I asked.

She smiled at me. "Oh, but I did. I called the tip line, but I never heard back, and the next I knew you'd charged David. So I didn't follow up. But tell me, Harry. How good of a job do you think you did of investigating Liz's murder? Did you make a rush to judgment?"

That was a tough one, but I answered her as honestly as I could. "Obviously not as good a job as I should have," I said. "A rush to judgment? There was enough evidence to charge him. A jury found him guilty. But, Janice, it's always easy to be wise after the fact. You're right, though. I don't think he did it either, which is why I'm trying to put things right."

"Janice, did you know Amy Murphy?" Kate asked.

Soames looked down at the floor, her hands clasped together

in front of her and said, "Amy…" She paused for a moment then said, "Yes, I knew her. She, too, was a friend. Not so much lately, but in the past. I heard what happened to her. She had a terrible drug habit. I thought she was clean, though."

"She was," Kate said. "More than fifteen years clean."

"So what happened, then?" She looked up at Kate.

"We don't know," Kate said, "but we're investigating it as a suspicious death."

"I haven't seen her in years," Soames said. "Last I heard, she was working at some diner."

"Was there anyone you know that might have wanted her out of the way? Someone who might have something to gain from her death?"

She leaned back in her chair, pursed her lips, thought for a minute, then shook her head and said, "Amy was… Let's say she was a little wild. She liked to experiment. She was also close to Liz. Very close. If Liz confided in anyone, it would have been Amy. As I said, it must be five years since I last spoke to her. I can't help you. I wish I could. I'm sorry."

I shook my head, then said, "We've taken up enough of your time, Ms. Soames. Thank you for your patience. You've been very helpful." I stood up, and so did Kate.

Soames also rose to her feet. She took two steps forward and offered me her hand. I shook it. Her grip was firm but soft, her skin cool.

"It was my pleasure, Mr. Starke," she said as she walked us to the door. "If I can help in any way at all, please call me. And good luck with your investigation. I hope you *are* able to set David free."

"So," Kate said, as we walked to the car. "She is quite a character."

"That she is," I said. "Unfortunately, other than confirming Reynolds had a high-profile, perverted client, we didn't learn very much, except that I did a damn poor job of the initial investigation."

"Don't be too hard on yourself, Harry," she said. "As you said, you had the evidence you needed, so you were justified in charging him. And you were under pressure to solve it quickly."

"Yes, but pressure from whom?" I replied. "That's the question. If we can find the answer to that, we may be close to a solution."

I looked at my watch. It was after twelve.

"I don't know about you," I said, "but I could do with something to eat, and we need to talk."

She nodded, shortened Samson's leash a little, then said, "Where d'you suggest?"

I looked at Samson, then at her and said, "Somewhere we can take him, I guess. You'd know better than me."

"Samson?" she said as she opened the rear door and he hopped inside. "I can take him almost anywhere. He's a K-9 officer, remember?"

29

WE OPTED FOR HANNIBAL'S ON HIXSON PIKE, AN INEXPENSIVE diner famous for its burgers.

We grabbed a booth at the north end of the restaurant and settled in. You don't go to Hannibal's for the extensive menu—they don't have one—just a variety of burgers to suit every taste, all featuring their signature Black Angus beef patties, with the exception, that is, of their veggie burger, which is on the menu more as a courtesy than a moneymaker.

I ordered the half-pounder with fried mushroom, lettuce, tomatoes and steak fries. Kate ordered… You guessed it: the Veggie Burger for her and two beef patties on the side for Samson. I looked at her in disgust.

"What?" she asked and took a sip of her half and half iced tea.

"How can you eat that?" I asked. "It's not natural."

"A girl's gotta watch her figure," she said, "especially at my age."

"You look fine to me," I said and could have bitten my tongue.

She simply smirked and took another sip of her tea.

Kate and I, we were once an item. Until I messed things up

and she dumped me. It took us both a long time to get past it, but we did, and ever since I've made it a point never to say anything to her that might be taken as suggestive. That being said, I slip up from time to time, as I did then. It meant nothing, but it wasn't something I consciously ever did.

"So," I said as we waited for our food. "Any word from your team?"

"Yes, as it happens, there is," she replied. "Corbin and Hawk talked to Bob Williams. Tracy and Cooper talked to Shirley Walker's husband, Chester, and Councilman Walter Keighley. Ah, here we go," she said as the waiter put our plates down in front of us and asked if we needed anything. We didn't, so he nodded and left.

Samson, by then, was on his feet and sniffing the air. Kate handed him his patties on a paper plate she'd had folded in her purse. They were gone in two huge bites, and she told him to lie down and behave, and he did, though he looked a little chagrined.

"She took a bite of her veggie burger and I watched in horror as she chewed contentedly with her eyes closed.

"Ewe!" I said and took a bite of mine. You have no idea how good it was. I don't know if it was because I was hungry, but I swear it was as good as any I'd ever had. The meat was topped with a single, bun-size Portobello mushroom cooked to perfection.

We ate in silence for several minutes before Kate finally put her veggie burger down, though there wasn't much left of it, and said, "As I was saying, Corbin and Hawk talked to Bob Williams, MaryAnn's ex-husband. He was out the night Reynolds was murdered. He says he remembers going to the store for cigarettes, but he wasn't gone more than thirty-minutes. His wife came in ten minutes after he did."

"Did they believe him?" I asked.

"Hawk certainly didn't," she replied and took a sip of her tea, "but then, Hawk rarely believes anybody, so that's no indication. Corbin has an open mind, but he's always ready to give the benefit of the doubt. What d'you think, Harry?"

"I wish I'd been there," I said, "but I'd trust Hawk's instincts. I've known him a long time. He's a master at reading body language. If he says the guy is lying, then he probably is. What about the other two?"

"Not much there, I'm afraid," she said. "Neither of them can remember what they were doing in 2001, much less on July 12 between nine and eleven. Councilman Keighley was outraged that we even asked him, though he admitted he knew Lana Baudette, but only through his philanthropic activities, fundraisers and the like."

"That's what Lana said," I replied. "How about Chester Walker?"

She shook her head. "No memory of that night. Nothing. Tracy said she believed him, but, well, you know how that goes. D'you think we should talk to him again?"

I made a face and shook my head. "Not right now," I said. "Geez, this thing is going nowhere pretty damn fast."

"What d'you want to do, Harry?" she asked.

"Phew… I dunno, Kate. I think maybe we should go to my office and see if Tim's come up with anything. That okay with you?"

She looked at her watch. It was a little after one. "I need to do something," she said. "So, yes, I guess."

"Oh," I said. "By the way, I have some news. It's kinda gotten lost, but Bob's coming back."

"Bob Ryan?" she almost shouted, loud enough for the people in the booths back and front to wake up and take notice. Then she calmed down and mouthed, "Bob Ryan?"

I grinned at her and nodded. I knew she'd be happy to hear it.

She and Bob had had a short-lived fling back in the day. It had ended by mutual agreement on good terms.

"He's coming back to work?" she asked.

Again, I nodded. "So he says," I replied.

"When?" she asked.

"The week after next," I replied.

"Geez," she said. "That *is* good news. D'you have a place for him?"

"I do, and here's the weird thing. I'd said to Jacque only a couple of days earlier that we needed to hire another… investigator…"

I paused, looked at her, and, for the umpteenth time, said, "I don't suppose you would consider…"

She shook her head and grinned.

"I didn't think so," I said with a sigh. "Though I can't think why not. I'd pay you double what they're paying you now. Oh well, never mind. Anyway, as I said, I'd only said a couple of days earlier that we need to hire someone when, out of the blue, he calls Jacque. Apparently, he's taken early retirement."

"But he was station chief in Kabul, wasn't he?" she asked. "And they let him go?"

"He was," I said. "Somewhere like that. And yes, they let him go. Anyway, I thought you'd like that. Maybe you and—"

"Oh, no!" she snapped. "Don't even go there. I'm quite happy with Thomas, thank you. Let's go if we're going. Come on, Sammy. Out of the way. On your feet, please. On second thought, Harry, I think I'll go back to the office. It's the end of the month and I have loads of paperwork to catch up on. So, if you'll run us back, please."

"Oh, shit!" I said. "I forgot that it's the end of the month. I have at least a dozen reports to go through. Jacque will have my… Yes, of course. Good plan. Let's go."

30

It was almost two when I arrived back at the office that afternoon and I was right. Jacque was waiting for me, and she was pissed."

"So," she said, her hands, no, fists, on her hips. "You decided to come back den? Well, don't even t'ink about goin' home until I have those reports in my hands."

"Of course not, my love," I said, and grabbed her by the shoulders, kissed her on the cheek and stepped back and grinned at her.

"That, Harry Starke, was totally, I mean totally, inappropriate. I shall file a complaint against you for sexual harassment with HR."

"We don't have HR," I said, still grinning.

"Well, den, I shall file a complaint with the boss."

"And that would be me," I said, grinning even wider. "C'mere!" And I reached out to grab her again, but she squealed with laughter and ran from the reception area. I ran after her, leaving Lucy smiling and shaking her head.

I caught up with her in the breakroom where TJ was pouring

coffee. She grabbed his arm and circled around behind him, peeping out from under his arm.

"What the hell?" he said.

"It's Harry," she said, laughing. "He's harassing me."

"All right," I said, "That's enough frivolity. We have work to do."

"Spoil sport," Jacque said petulantly as she came out from behind TJ.

I winked at her, and she blushed. "Where's Tim?" I asked.

"Where d'you t'ink he is?" she asked. "He's sequestered in that dark hell hole he calls his office. You want me to get him for you?"

"Yeah, but I need coffee first," I said. "I'm going to make a fresh pot."

"Go sit yourself down," she said. "I'll make it and bring it to you. You go to your office and get on with those reports."

And I did, though I hadn't been there but a few minutes when Tim walked in grinning like the proverbial Cheshire cat, loaded up with laptop, iPad, and phone.

"What're you so happy about?" I asked.

"Bob's coming back," he said. "I still can't believe it."

"Be careful what you wish for," I said, remembering the cryptic message I received when he left. *Still,* I thought, *he was there when I needed him, though how the hell he found out I was in trouble... I'll have to ask him.*

"So," I said. "What have you got for me, Tim?"

"Is it okay if I sit down?" he asked and sat down before I could answer.

I gave him the look. He responded with a grin and set his laptop and iPad down on my desk.

"You asked me to look into one Brendan Loftin, and I did," he said. "Strangely enough, he was easy to track down. I just did a search of the name—it's not too common you know—and voila, up she comes… he comes. Brendan's a he. Not a she. I mean—"

He caught my look, smiled self-consciously, put his hand over his mouth, coughed, did that thing with his glasses, and finally continued, "Loftin is a bit of a nomad, a wanderer, if you get what I mean. He's been around the block. So, I found him online. He'd listed himself on that recruiting app, ZipRecruiter. I was able to download his resume. Oh yeah, he's been around. He's forty-three. He graduated from Brainerd High School in 1997 and went to work for HLC as a laborer. That lasted two years until April of '99 when he went to work at Jackson Chair. That lasted a year. He quit and went hiking. After that, he had a couple of odd jobs until he went to work as a PA for Vickie Keighley, a woman highly esteemed in the community. Now, how he got that job is a mystery to me. Still, that lasted from May 2001 until December 2015, when she let him go just in time for Christmas. How considerate of her. Since then he's…"

It was at that point, I stopped paying attention. He was boring the hell out of me. *Vickie Keighley?* I thought. *Has to be a coincidence, I suppose.*

"Vickie Keighley?" I asked, interrupting his diatribe.

He frowned at me, looked surprised, then said, "Yes. He served as her personal assistant at her real estate company. Why she let him go isn't clear—"

"D'you have an address for him?" I asked as Jacque stepped inside with two cups of coffee.

He looked up at her and said, "Oooh goodie. Is one of those for me?"

She gave him a withering look and said, "No, they're for me and Harry. Go get your own." And she set one of the cups down in front of me.

"Well, slap me down with a cactus flower," he said. "Is that the way to treat a gifted and valued employee, sir?" He looked at me for support.

I gave him a big smile and said, "That address, gifted and valued employee?"

"Well, er… no," he said. "Not actually. The one on his resume is old, a rental apartment. I checked; he left there four years ago. The phone number doesn't work either. I did find this photo of him on social media. It was pretty recent, taken at a bowling alley. The caption says he's an assistant manager. See the bowling alley logo on his polo shirt?"

"Yeah, well," I said. "Don't worry about it for now. I need to get these reports done for Jacque." By then, she'd seated herself. She smiled sweetly at me and sipped her coffee.

"Go on, Tim," I said. "Get out of here, and well done, as usual. You are indeed a gifted and valued employee. Don't let it go to your head."

The end of the month reports are always a bear. They are not something I can skip through and just sign off on. The IRS would love that.

"Jacque," I said after Tim had closed the door behind him, "Don't worry, I'll hand these off to TJ as soon as I've finished. Give me an hour, maybe two, okay?"

She sighed, then nodded and said, "I'll hold your calls and see that you're not disturbed. You know where I'll be if you need me."

I nodded absently, and she left.

But buckling down to the mundane task was easier said than done. We had several cases in various stages of progress, but my mind kept drifting back to the one in hand. I struggled on until at twenty-minutes to five I closed the last file, flopped back in my chair and closed my eyes, and there I remained in a semi-conscious state for at least ten more minutes. Finally, I opened my eyes, picked up the phone and buzzed Jacque.

"Come and get 'em," I said and returned the phone to its cradle.

"I don't want company," I said pointedly as she picked up the files.

"Grumpy old man," she said as she closed the door behind her.

I wanted out of there. I wanted to go home. I needed a drink. But most of all, I needed to think. We'd been working the Archer case for almost ten days, and where were we?

I heaved a deep breath, shook my head, and closed my eyes again. According to the people we'd talked to so far, only a couple of things were clear: the only real suspect we had was an unknown client who liked rough sex. And we had three cops who were, at the time, on the take in one form or another. It's true we had several persons of interest that either didn't have an alibi or no memory of what they were doing that fateful day. I also knew Reynolds' killer was still alive and out there somewhere and that Murphy's death was somehow tied to the Reynolds case, but how? That was the question I needed an answer to. And that answer was as elusive as the sasquatch.

Well, we still have Loftin to talk to, I thought. *Maybe he can provide an answer.* It was a thought, but I had little confidence that it would turn anything up. I decided I'd go to the bowling alley at eleven the following morning when they opened.

And what about Finkle and Whacker? I thought, *Whacker's retired, so there's not much can be done there. But Finkle? He needs to be shut down. He also knows more than he's telling. I think maybe we should talk to him again, this time with the chief present.*

I looked at my watch. It was five-fifteen. I gave it up, cleared my desk and went downstairs and went to see Jacque in her office.

"I've had it," I said. "I'm going home. Don't call me. I'll call you. I need some quality family time for a change. I need to mend some fences."

31

I WAS HOME BY SIX THAT EVENING, AND I DID SPEND SOME quality time with Jade and Amanda, though it was somehow lacking that extra little spark. We went for a long walk under the streetlights up to the Incline Railway station and watched the carriages coming and going and the twinkling lights of the city below. I ended up carrying Jade back to the house when she cried that her little legs were hurting. It was a nice evening, but I admit I was a little pre-occupied; my bad.

And, of course, I had another restless night. We went to bed early, around ten, my first mistake. My second was lying there, tossing and turning. In the end, I gave it up, got out of bed, and went downstairs where I made coffee, put on an old Navy Peacoat and went outside onto the patio.

The night was chilly, the sky clear, stars bright, and there was a waxing moon to the south. I stood for a moment at the wall, cup in hand, staring down at the city lights. It's a view that never gets old. Then I sat down on one of the teak chaises. I drank my coffee and made a conscious effort to clear the crap out of my mind. And it must have worked, for three hours later, at seven o'clock, Amanda woke me with a cup of coffee.

"So," she said, smiling as she set the cup down on the floor beside me, "you prefer this to me, do you?"

It wasn't the first time I'd fallen asleep like that, and it wasn't the last.

"You know better than that," I said, taking her hand and pulling her down.

I kissed her. She spluttered, made a face, and said, "Ugh. Morning breath."

I grinned at her, sat up, swung my legs off the chaise, stood up, stretched, reached down, grabbed the cup and said, "What's for breakfast?"

She made another face, then said, "It's your turn to make it, sailor."

"No sailor, honey," I replied. "No military at all. I was a cop. Remember?"

"How about I make my special scrambled eggs?" I said.

"Sounds like a plan," she replied. "But you'd better get a shower first. Maria will be here to get Jade ready for school in a minute."

"Then I'd better hurry," I said.

By eight o'clock each of us, even Jade, was ready to face the day, and what a day it was about to be.

I made it into the office by eight-thirty. It was a new month, my slate was relatively clear, and I was feeling kinda chipper. I said good morning to Lucy, hugged Jacque—much to her feigned disgust—poured myself a cup of coffee and called everyone to my office for a chat.

Now a chat at my company is an informal meeting where everyone gets to say whatever it is they're thinking. I do it quite often, especially when I'm looking for inspiration, and it works. Electronics are not allowed; phones must be turned off. Tim hates that, but that works, too: no distractions.

We gathered on the two couches that flanked the massive

coffee table and when we were all sitting comfortably, I said, "The subject is the Elizabeth Reynolds case."

The reaction was a chorus of groans.

"I know, I know," I said, "but it's the most pressing case in hand. We've spent ten days chasing it and, as far as I can tell, we have nothing. I need ideas. Who wants to go first?"

The question was met with complete silence.

"I see," I said. "No one! Okay, I'll go first. Kate and I are going to see if we can track down Brendan Loftin at the bowling alley when we get done here."

TJ surreptitiously looked at his watch.

"You got somewhere to be, Marine?" I asked.

"I've always got somewhere to be, *Captain*," he said sarcastically. "Is this going to take long?"

"As long as it takes," I replied.

"Okay," he growled. "Here's an idea for you. Why don't you let me go talk to Finkle again, by myself, and squeeze him? All I need is five minutes alone with him."

"Oooh, can I watch?" Tim said, grinning.

"No, you frickin' can't," I said to TJ, though the idea had some appeal. I had no doubt that five minutes with TJ would make anyone squeal. "You want to get arrested, and me along with you?"

He shrugged, looked at his watch again, and then settled back on the couch and folded his arms across his chest.

"Any more bright ideas?" I asked, dryly.

"What *are* we going to do about Finkle?" Heather asked. "We all know he's dirty as a pig in a mud puddle."

"That's not our problem," I said, though I'd been thinking much the same myself.

Heather shook her head, then said, "So, where exactly are we with the case?"

I looked at her, my brain whirling, searching for an answer.

"Truthfully?" I said. "We have nothing but an alibi for the guy that I convicted of the crime, and a half-dozen persons of interests who either have no alibi or don't remember if they do or not, and one dark suspect no one can put a name too. That's it. We've interviewed everyone but Loftin. Amy Murphy's dead. The case is twenty-one years cold. I need help here, people."

But help wasn't forthcoming. They were all as much in the dark as I was. I finally wrapped it up at nine and sent them on their way. Now it was my turn to clock watch. I had ninety minutes to burn before Kate was due to arrive, so I decided to give her a call.

"Hey," I said when she answered. "What are you doing?"

"Funny you should ask," she said. "I have a couple of things I need to wrap up here, then I'm heading your way. I have something I need to discuss with you."

"Oh yeah?" I said, my interest piqued. "And what's that?"

"Not over the phone, Harry," she replied.

"Okay," I said. "I'll see you when I see you."

What could it be she couldn't discuss over the phone? I wondered.

I soon found out, for she and Samson walked into my office thirty minutes later and she had a manila file in her hand. And again, my interest piqued.

"Whatcha got there?" I asked as she pushed the door shut behind her.

"And hello to you, too," she said, snarkily. "You, my curious friend, need to bone up on your manners."

I grinned at her and said, "I'll have you know my manners are impeccable, thanks to my dear old mom."

"If that's true," she replied, "they're slipping and in dire need of an overhaul."

"Oh come on, Kate. Stop fooling around. What d'you have?"

"I have," she said as she sat down on the couch lately vacated by TJ and Heather, "these." She opened the file and took out a thick stack of paper and handed them to me, retaining the top one.

I looked at them, frowned, and said, "Bank records?"

"Yep," she said, and handed me the one she'd retained. "Look at the name."

"Henry Finkle? Geez, Kate, you haven't—"

"No," she said, cutting me off. "Jack has, which is why I couldn't mention it over the phone. He did it without me knowing. If he gets found out, Johnston will fire him."

"So why'd he do it?" I asked. "And what do they prove?"

"I'm not sure, which is why I need your opinion." She leaned forward, put her elbows on her knees, clasped her hands together in front of her, nodded at the stack of papers, and said, "Jack says the numbers don't add up; whatever that means. He hacked Henry's bank records—"

"Sounds like Tim," I said, smiling, cutting her off.

She gave me one of her "looks" and continued, "He went into the bank's archives. I didn't know that was even possible. He went all the way back to 2000."

She paused and made a face that narrowed her eyes, stretched her mouth and showed her teeth. It wasn't a pretty sight. "He also did… Gordon Whacker."

"Oh shit," I said. "What is he? Suicidal?"

She shook her head and said, "I had him delete Whacker's stuff. He was clean, but Henry…" Again she nodded at the papers in my hand. "He… may or may not be."

"Okay," I said, "you're going to have to explain. I don't have time or the expertise to analyze these kinds of numbers."

"From December 2000 all the way to July 2001, there are monthly cash deposits of one-thousand dollars. I say cash, but it doesn't say that. They are just deposits, and they could be for anything, a moonlight security job, for instance. You know how that goes. But then, in September, the deposits increased from one thousand to twenty-five hundred. That was a lot of money for a security job in 2001. But then, in July 2002, they stopped; June was the last deposit. No more extraneous deposits. What d'you think? Can't be a coincidence, can it?"

I stared at her, pursed my lips, and slowly shook my head. "I don't know what to say," I replied. "I need to think about it."

"Someone was paying him off, Harry."

I nodded. I had no doubt she was right, but who was it?

"Okay," I said, finally. "We need to keep this to ourselves for now. If… when this gets out it's going to make some waves, a frickin' tsunami. You need to tell Jack to cover his ass. Johnston's going to want to know where we got this, and his first thought is going to be Tim, and his second Jack."

"I already told him," she said and began to bite on one of her thumbnails.

"We need more answers," I said. "We ruffle the wrong feathers, it could get someone killed.

"We are going to have to talk to him, but not in the department. Somewhere quiet, out of the way, where we can't be overheard. That's on you. In the meantime, we need to find Loftin. Let's get out of here. We can talk on the way."

She nodded, but then, as I reached out to grab the doorknob, she put a hand on my arm and said, "Harry, Henry knows who killed Elizabeth. I can feel it in my bones. Those deposits are hush money. He was covering for someone right up until she was murdered and then, the month after, the payments increased from a grand to two-and-a-half. When was Archer convicted?"

I didn't have to think about it. The same thoughts had been whirling around inside my own head.

"Wednesday, June 22, 2002," I said.

"Geez," was all she said.

"Yeah," I said, "geez!"

I was, by then, in no mood to go chasing down Brendan

Loftin, but I needed space, time to think. It could not be a coincidence. Well, it could, but my gut was telling me it wasn't. So, I decided to stick to the plan and drive to the bowling alley, where I assumed he worked, and if he didn't, I figured they might be able to tell us where we could find him.

I waved at Jacque on the way out and, keys in hand, followed by Kate, I almost ran down the three steps. My car was perhaps a hundred feet from the front entrance, and I was maybe a third of the way there with Kate close behind when Jacque came through the door and yelled, "Harry!"

I stopped, turned around, swung my arm around my back and clicked the button on the key fob to unlock the car door and... *KABAM!* I was lifted off my feet and thrown across the parking lot by an enormous explosion.

I landed flat on my face, rolled across the parking lot, debris raining down around me.

For what seemed like an age, I lay there, literally stunned, my head pounding, my ears ringing.

Kate! I thought.

I struggled to my knees. *What... Frickin'... Oh shit!*

I looked around. My Range Rover had been reduced to a blazing heap of scrap metal, a black cloud of smoke rising into the air. The cars on either side, one of them Jacque's, were burning, blazing fiercely.

Kate was lying on her back.

I scrambled to my feet, staggered over to her and dropped to my knees beside her. Her eyes were closed. Her mouth was slightly open. *She's breathing. Thank God!* I thought.

I looked up. Jacque was nowhere to be seen, but then the door opened and she ran out, followed by Lucy, and then Heather and TJ. *She must have been blown back inside,* I thought as I looked down at Kate, not knowing what to do.

Then, as if she'd received an electric shock, her eyes opened wide, and she coughed violently.

"Is she all right?" Jacque yelled.

"Somebody call an ambulance," I shouted.

But Heather already had her phone to her ear.

"Harry, you're bleeding like a pig," TJ said as he grabbed my arm and pulled me to my feet and steered me away.

I barely heard him over the ringing in my ears. "What… the hell… happened?" I mumbled, my head spinning.

"Somebody put a bomb in your car," TJ said.

"What?"

"A bomb," he shouted. "In your car. You're one lucky son of a bitch, Harry. Five steps closer and it would have shredded you and Kate."

"Kate?" I said and pulled my arm free. "Kate?"

I turned around. She was sitting up, Jacque at one side, Heather at the other, Samson inches away behind her. Her face was white. Blood was trickling down her face from a cut on her forehead. She looked up at me.

"What the hell happened, Harry?" she asked, pushing Jacque and Heather away.

"I'm okay," she said to Jacque. "Wow!" She was breathing heavily. "I'm fine. Just give me a hand up, please."

They helped her to her feet. She wiped the blood from her eye with the back of her hand, looked at the burning cars, and said, "Geez. Somebody really doesn't like you, Harry."

"What?" I shouted.

She just shook her head and began to check herself over.

I looked around the lot. There wasn't much left of my car. The other two were burning fiercely. The lot and the road beyond were littered with debris. Several of the windows across the street were shattered. I looked behind me at my building. The windows were all intact.

Thanks to the armored glass, I thought as my head began to clear.

"You're lucky to be alive, Harry," I heard Jacque say faintly. "Kate, too."

I felt something wet in the palm of my hand. I looked down. It was Samson licking me. There was not a mark on him.

"You're bleeding, Harry," TJ repeated. I could still barely hear him for the ringing in my ears.

"Where?" I said, still somewhat dazed.

"Your thigh," he replied. "Your pants. They're soaked."

I looked down. He was right. Not only were they soaked, but they were also torn. I leaned forward and with two fingers I pulled the cloth gently away and—

"Don't touch it," TJ snapped, grabbing my arm and pulling my hand away. "You don't know how far it's in there or what damage it's done."

I looked down at the jagged piece of metal sticking out of my left inner thigh and my mind went blank.

I shook my head, looked at TJ, then again at the hunk of metal. "Geez," I said. "You don't think?"

"I don't think anything," he replied. "It's best not to take chances. The medics are on the way."

Now, I'm sure you can imagine the chaos of the next forty-eight hours. I could try to describe it, but how do you describe something like that? You've seen those news reports where the interviewee says something like, "it was like a bomb went off," or, "It was like a war zone?" Well, a bomb did go off. Neither statement does it any kind of justice. There's simply no way to adequately describe being in the middle of a bomb blast. It's just… flabbergasting.

Fortunately, my worst fears were not realized. The chunk of metal had been driven deep into my leg, but it had missed the femoral artery. Some stitches and a stern warning to take some time off and the hospital doctor turned me loose. I heeded the warning, sort of, and took the rest of the day, and the next day, off and returned to work on Thursday.

Kate was, as she said, fine. The cut to her forehead was deep and, despite the best efforts of a plastic surgeon friend of mine, it did leave a faint scar. Thomas Drews, her fella, took her home, and the next day she was, of course, back at work.

Me? It took almost a week before the ringing in my ears abated, but I, too, was back at work two days later.

As to the damage… Sheesh, you have no idea. They could have carted what was left of my Range Rover away in a wheelbarrow. As it was, they loaded it onto a low-loader and hauled it off for forensic examination. It was later determined that the bomb was a one-pound block of C-4 rigged to the electronic door locks. As TJ said, I was one lucky SOB. Had Jacque not called out to me; had I not stopped walking when I did, I would surely have been killed by the blast; Kate, too.

Only one of the seven vehicles in the lot escaped damage. All had suffered from the blast to one degree or another. Jacque's Subaru was reduced to a burned-out hulk, as was Lucy's Kia Soul. The rear window of Tim's Jeep Wrangler was shattered. Heather's CRV looked as if it had been peppered with machine gun fire. TJ, always fearful of damage done to his 2015 Corvette by other cars, had parked it at the far end of the lot, and thus it was spared blast damage. Kate's cruiser parked two empty spaces away to the left of Jacque's car was shielded from the blast but suffered extensive paint damage from the heat of the fire.

So, as you can imagine, chaos reigned over my office complex for the next week and beyond. The parking lot was a crime scene, and thus taped off. Fortunately, there was a rear entrance, so we were not denied access to our offices.

My insurance adjuster was not allowed near the car and had to photograph the remains from afar, along with Jacque's, Tim's and

Heather's, who were all insured by the same company. Lucy, having only lately joined us, was with another company. Needless to say, I made sure they all had rental cars. TJ's Corvette was released the same day. Me? I received the go ahead to replace my Rover the next day.

It's easy to make light of it now, but believe me when I tell you it was… an indescribably horrific event. One I'll never forget. But, to use a worn-out cliché, when all was said and done, all was well, except for… Amanda. Oh, boy!

She arrived at the hospital while I was being stitched up. I took one look at her face, squeezed my eyes tight shut and waited for the second blast. It didn't come. What did come was a tearful five minutes. Now I have a tough time with tears. I would much rather she rant and rave, which, by the way, she never does; never has. But, after what we've been through together, and all the promises I've made and broken, she's still hanging in there. Wow! What a woman! And no, she didn't insist I quit, but she did insist on an explanation for what had happened, but I didn't have one. She held my hand throughout the repairs to my leg and then drove me home.

Then there was the media. Hah! I avoided them as best I could, at least until the next day when I woke to find all three major outlets camped out on East Brow just beyond my gates. I gave them a brief speech explaining I had no idea why, what, or who, and that the investigation was ongoing. It seemed to satisfy them because, by noon, they were all gone.

I also received a call from Thomas Drews, Kate's boyfriend. He asked if he could interview me for his true crime podcast. I told him I'd think about it. Had it been anyone else, I'd have told him to go screw himself. As it was, I figured I owed Kate at least that much.

Finally, and toughest of all, was the inevitable interview with Chief Johnston. He was not happy. In fact, he was seriously pissed. He'd almost lost his best detective, and that did not go down well, especially when we told him we were no closer to a solution. Had it not been for the murder of Amy Murphy, I think he would have shut us down. As it was, Kate told him it was one of the hazards of the job. To which, he had no alternative but to agree. Then he glared at me and told us both to get it sorted, and quick.

What could I say to that? I didn't. I kept my mouth shut, and he didn't pursue it further, much to my relief. He could've had my license revoked.

32

AND SO I TOOK WEDNESDAY OFF, SORT OF. I MADE SOME CALLS, most of them to my people. Well, what was I supposed to do? We were all victims of the car bomb, to one degree or another. I had to make sure their needs were provided for. I also needed to make sure at least something was happening with the investigation, so I had TJ and Heather go hunt for Brendan Loftin. That was on Wednesday.

So, by nine-thirty on Wednesday morning, I was done for the day, and relieved to be so. Maria had taken Jade to school. The house was empty, the wound to my leg painful but bearable. I was in a weird mood, grateful, I suppose, for the escape I'd had the day before. I'd had some near things before, too many to count, some of them close calls, but nothing quite like that bomb blast, although the Calaway Jones thing was pretty traumatic. I don't think Amanda ever really got over that one.

I looked at her across the kitchen table and told her I was sorry, then I took her hand and led her back upstairs. We spent the rest of the morning in bed together. It was… wonderful. One of those precious moments that happen only a few times in a lifetime, and I'm sure it was because of my almost miraculous escape. Whatever it was, it ended with Amanda weeping softly in my arms.

~

I RETURNED TO WORK, against Amanda's wishes, the following day, Thursday, thinking I would get some work done, but it wasn't to be. A cloud hung over my team like a wet blanket. Understandable, I think. It was the second time we'd been the victims of a bombing. A bomb planted by my old, now deceased nemesis, Lester Tree, had destroyed our offices on Georgia Avenue.

Be that as it may, there was work to do. And questions to be answered. Of those, the big one was who? Who planted the bomb in my car?

But all was quiet. I felt as if my people were afraid to talk to me. Of course, I was wrong. They were just trying to give me some space.

I'd arrived at eight-thirty, as usual, and began trying to catch up on the ever-mounting paperwork. By two-thirty that afternoon, I'd had enough, and I called Heather and TJ into my office.

"So, tell me," I said, without preamble. "What about Brendan Loftin?"

Heather looked at TJ. He shrugged, then said, "We went to the bowling alley, as you said. He wasn't there. But, on questioning the manager, we learned he's employed as an assistant manager, and that he was supposed to be at work that day but hadn't shown up. We questioned several of the employees. They said it wasn't like him, and that he hadn't taken a sick day in the two-and-a-half years he'd worked there. He's a popular guy. The manager gave us his address. We went there. It was a ratty little apartment on the south side. He wasn't there. That was at one in the afternoon. I went back at seven-thirty last night. No sign of him. So that was yesterday. I called the manager this morning, and he still hasn't showed up. I think the guy's gone missing."

Yeah, I thought. *Me, too.*

I looked at them both as I bit my thumbnail. "We need to find him," I said.

"I agree," TJ replied, "but how the hell are we going to do that?"

Good question, I thought, and another one I didn't have an answer to as thoughts of bombs and drug overdoses danced through my head.

"Guys," I said, "I have a sneaky feeling someone is one step ahead of us. First Amy Murphy, then me, now Loftin."

I thought for a minute, then said, "We need answers. We need to find this guy. What about his past employers? How about the Keighley woman? Tim said he worked for her for what, fifteen years?"

"You mean Vickie Keighley," Heather said, after consulting her notes. "Apparently, he worked for her from 2001 until 2015. She runs a successful real estate agency. Her husband is Walter Keighley, city councilman. Maybe TJ and I should go talk to her."

"Maybe," I said. "But first, I have something to share with you." And I told them what Kate had discovered about Henry Finkle. I'd been thinking about it ever since the bombing, and I thought it was about time they knew.

"Geez, Harry," TJ said. "You gotta turn me loose on that guy."

I smiled at him and shook my head. "Not until we have all our ducks in a row. I don't want any of you getting arrested. For now, keep what I've told you to yourselves. Henry's time will come, I promise."

It was at that moment my phone rang. It was Kate. I put her on speaker.

"Harry," she said, after the usual greetings, "I hate to spoil your day again, but we've found Loftin. He's dead. Some homeless guy found him in an alley with his throat cut."

"Damn!" I snapped. "You're sure it's him?"

"Oh yeah. We found his wallet. The driver's license is his. The photo matches. It's him all right."

"Damn, damn, damn," I muttered. Once again, the rug had been pulled out from under our feet.

"What are you going to do, Harry?" Kate asked.

"Hell, I don't know, do I? Our killer always seems to be one step ahead of us. When did he die, d'you know?"

"Last night, between ten and midnight, so Doc said," she replied.

"The bowling alley," I muttered.

"What?" Kate asked. "Speak up. I can't hear you."

"The bowling alley," I repeated. "TJ and Heather went looking for him there yesterday. That must be how our killer found out we were looking for him."

I looked at TJ. He shrugged but said nothing. Heather also said nothing.

"I gotta go, Kate. Stay in touch. I'll call you if anything breaks." And I hung up.

"Now we're really at a dead end," I said. "We're fast running out of prospects. I guess we need to talk to the Keighley woman. See if she can shed any light on anything." I looked at my watch. It was almost noon.

I shook my head in frustration. "Damn it!" I muttered and heaved a sigh. "Go on, get out of here," I said. "We'll figure something out in the morning."

33

It was just after seven when I finally arrived home that evening. Maria was upstairs putting Jade to bed, and Amanda was cleaning up the kitchen.

"Hey, you," I said as I walked in and dropped my rental car keys on the counter.

"Hey, yourself," she replied truculently. "I wonder why you bother to come home at all sometimes."

"Yeah, I know, and I'm sorry," I said. "Something came up and—"

"Something *always* comes up," she said, "but you didn't call, and I've been worried about you all day."

I stepped up behind her, took her shoulders, and turned her around. She looked up into my eyes. I kissed her.

"I'm sorry, sweetheart," I said. "I really am. I don't know what I was thinking."

She didn't answer. Instead, she pushed me gently away, walked to the oven, grabbed a glove, took out a pan of lasagna and set it down on the table.

"I waited for you," she said. "You want red or white?"

"White, I guess. How was your day?"

"Pretty damn crappy, since you ask," she said as she poured the wine. "You were almost killed, Harry, and you didn't think to call to let me know how… Oh, what's the use? You'll never change."

She grabbed a serving spoon and carved out a huge chunk of lasagna and dumped it on the plate and set it down in front of me. "You want more," she said, "you get it yourself."

She carved a much smaller portion for herself and sat down and stared at it, then pushed it away. "I'm not hungry," she said.

She was in a mood, and I could hardly blame her. I also knew better than to talk when she's like that, so I said nothing. I *was* hungry, and as the lasagna was homemade, I knew it would be good. And it was.

By nine o'clock, though, she'd come around, and I was forgiven with a warning to be more thoughtful in the future, to which I heartily agreed, thankful to be out of the proverbial doghouse.

~

I SLEPT SOUNDLY THAT NIGHT, though why, I don't know. I went to bed with my mind in a whirl. Be that as it may, as soon as my head hit the pillow, I went out like a light, to rise refreshed and ready to go at six-thirty. It was too late to go for a run and too cold to swim, so I spent fifteen minutes in the basement on the elliptical, and then I took Amanda a cup of coffee.

An hour later, I was out of the house and heading down the mountain wondering what the day held in store. Had I only known—

The first thing I did when I arrived at the office was call the weekly Friday morning conference. That took just twenty minutes, the next fifteen minutes was spent with Jacque, and the third to clear my desktop of the detritus of a wholly unproductive week. By then it was just after nine. I called Heather and TJ to my office and sent them out to interview the Keighley's, then I called Kate.

Kate was in a better mood than I was, having spent the night at home with Thomas Drews. *That relationship seems to be progressing nicely,* I thought absentmindedly. She ended the call by telling me she'd call me later when she'd gotten her own team sorted out. And so, I settled back in my chair, determined to think this thing through and come to some sort of decision.

It was almost time, so I thought, to call it quits with what we had and go to the DA. And that… Well, I had no illusions about it. David's alibi, provided after twenty-one years by his lover, wasn't enough to get him a new trial, much less a reprieve or a commutation, but I'd just about had it. We were two weeks in. Kate and I had almost been killed. It had cost me a small fortune in time and resources, and we still had virtually nothing. Yes, there was a killer out there, and he, or she, had to be caught, but that was the PD's job. They were far better equipped to handle it than I was. Was it time to call it a day and cut my losses? I was beginning to think so.

And then, about an hour later, I received a call from Heather to tell me they were at the Keighley's home, but there was no one there. And then she said, "So we decided to go to her real estate office, but there was no one there either. The door was locked, and the lights were off, which was kinda strange because the sign on the door said they opened at nine. It's now five after ten. What d'you want us to do?"

"Okay," I said with a sigh. "Come on back." And it was at that moment I finally decided to call it off. But then I began to think about it. It was Friday morning. There was no one home and there was no one at her busy real estate office, and that made no sense. There's always someone at a real estate office. The associates take turns at the walk-ins. *What's up with that?* I wondered.

"Heather, you and I are going back to that real estate office. TJ, you stay there."

~

WE TOOK Heather's car and it was almost noon when we arrived outside the Keighley's real estate office on Broad. The door was still locked, but the lights were on. So I hammered on the door, at first to no avail. But I kept at it and, eventually, she came bustling out from the back to the door.

She glared at me through the glass and mouthed, "We're closed. Go away."

I shook my head and held up my PI badge so she could see it. She squinted at it, locked eyes with me, then nodded and opened the door.

"Who are you?" she snapped. "What do you want? Can't you see we're closed?"

"My name's Harry Starke," I said, smiling at her. "I'm a private investigator. This is my associate Heather Stillwell—"

"I have nothing to say to you," she snapped, cutting me off and starting to close the door.

I put my hand on the door and said, "I just have a couple of questions. It won't take but a minute."

"I said I have nothing to say. Now please go away."

I nodded, but didn't remove my hand from the door. "I understand," I said, "and if you'd rather talk to the police instead—"

"Police?" she said, cutting me off. "What? Why? What are you talking about?"

"Just a few minutes, I promise," I said.

She stared at me for several seconds, then nodded, reluctantly, I thought, and then she pulled the door open and backed away, and we stepped inside.

She was a somewhat diminutive woman of indeterminate age,

mostly because of the cosmetic work she'd had done. I pegged her to be in her mid-sixties, though she could have been younger. She was five-three…ish, but wearing four-inch heels that raised her up to around five-eight. Her hair had been dyed blonde, almost white. Her neck was stretched so tight I could see the tendons. Her face was small, heart-shaped, and smooth—not a wrinkle—and she was heavily made up. The hazel eyes glittered in the artificial light, and I figured she must be wearing contacts. And she was wearing what appeared to be an expensively tailored, tan business trouser suit.

"I've told you, I've nothing to say," she repeated for the third time.

"I haven't told you why we're here yet," I said.

That seemed to take her aback a little. "Well… what is it, then?" she snapped.

"We'd like to talk to you about Brendan Loftin," I said. "He worked for you, I believe."

She frowned, then said, "That was years ago. What about him?"

"He's dead," I replied.

"Why am I not surprised?" she muttered. "Drugs, I suppose. The man was his own worst enemy. I fired him when I found him wasted in his office at ten o'clock one morning."

"Not drugs, ma'am," I replied. "He was found in an alley with his throat cut."

Her mouth dropped open. She was obviously stunned by the news. "Oh… my… God," she stammered. "No! Really?"

"Really," I said.

"When?" she asked.

"Wednesday," I replied. "Between ten and midnight. When did you last see him, Mrs. Keighley?"

"It's been… I don't know. Months… Three months, perhaps. He dropped by the office. We had a cup of coffee together. I always liked him. I just couldn't put up with his ways. My husband saw him last week, I believe. That's it. That's all I know. Now, would you please leave? I have work to do."

"Where are your people, Mrs. Keighley?" Heather asked. "It's kind of rare for a real estate practice to be… understaffed."

"What are you talking about, woman?" she snapped. "We're not understaffed. They are out doing the weekly caravan, visiting the new listings."

Heather made a face. I smiled.

"So, are we done?" she asked.

I thought for a moment, then said, "Did you also know Elizabeth Reynolds?"

Even through the makeup, I could see the color drain from her face. She stared at me for a moment, then glanced at Heather, then back at me.

"What about her?" she asked with a gulp.

Now that gave me pause for thought. She'd recognized the name instantly. She didn't ask me who she was. And, by the look on her face, I could tell she was… Let's say perturbed.

"I understand she was a… a friend of your husband's." I said, smiling gently at her.

At that, she visibly blanched and said, "I think you'd better come through to my office." She turned her back on us and walked off into a darkened corridor.

We followed. Heather first, then me, and, for the first time since Betty Markham walked into my office, I felt we were on to something.

"Please, sit down," she said as she closed the door behind her. And we did. We took our seats on the two high-back chairs strategically placed in front of her desk.

She stared at us across the desk. We waited for her to break the silence.

The wait became uncomfortable, and I was about to speak

when she said, "Elizabeth Reynolds was a prostitute, as I'm sure you already know, as you were the one who put her killer away, weren't you, Mr. Starke?"

She held up her hand before I could answer and continued, "Yes, I know who you are. Who doesn't? You have been featured on local television more times than I can count. Now let me say this to you: she was a prostitute. At the time of her death, there were vicious rumors circulating in high places that my husband was one of her clients. He wasn't. My husband, Mr. Starke, is many things, but he does not, nor has he ever, stooped so low as to associate with women of ill repute."

Women of ill repute? Now that was one I hadn't heard in many a long year, and I almost smiled at her, but I didn't. Instead, I simply sat there with my arms folded waiting for her to continue., and she did.

"My husband was then, and is now, a revered member of the city council. Such vicious rumors are detrimental to his good name and character, and to mine, I might add, and I will not have it. D'you hear? I… will… not… have it!"

"Nobody is accusing your husband of anything," Heather said gently. "All Mr. Starke did was ask you a simple question, which you have yet to answer. Was your husband friendly with Elizabeth Reynolds? No one is suggesting he was availing himself of her services, but she did move in somewhat exalted circles, so we've been led to understand. Her *friends*…" Heather stressed the word friends "…included many members of the city's upper class."

"Now look here, young lady," she snapped, and I had to smile at that. Heather's almost as old as I am. "I won't have this kind of talk," Keighley continued. "If I hear a single word of it, I shall sue you for slander. Now, I insist you leave. If you don't, I shall be forced to call the police."

"Please," I said, lightly, "feel free to do so, and be sure to ask for either Captain Gazzara or Chief Johnston. You see, they've reopened the Elizabeth Reynolds case and we've been asked to collaborate in the investigation. We believe that the murder of Brendan Loftin is connected to it, somehow, which is why we're here. You can cooperate with us, or you can talk to the police. An innocent man has spent the last twenty-one years in prison, and I, as you rightly say, was the one who put him there, and I'm determined to put it right. Now, I'd like to talk to your husband. Where is he?"

"Well, you can't," she replied, nastily. "He's not here. You can see that for yourself. He's never here. He's at home."

"He wasn't an hour ago," Heather said.

"Well, he was probably not answering the door," she said. "What is it you want with him, anyway?"

"I want to know where he was the night Elizabeth Reynolds was murdered," I said.

"He was at home," she replied, immediately and without thought. "With me. All night."

Now it was my turn to blanch. I frowned at her, and I could tell she knew by the look on my face that she'd made a mistake. "Well, I don't know that for sure," she said, "but as far as I can remember, that's where he was."

"I'm sure that's true," I said, mildly and with a smile. "I can't remember what I had for breakfast yesterday, let alone what I was doing more than twenty years ago. Who would?"

She smiled back at me and nodded.

"So where can I find him?" I asked gently, still smiling.

"As I said," she replied. "He should be at home. If not… Well, it is Friday. He could be at the country club, I suppose."

"Well," I said. "I think we've taken up enough of your time. We'll be off now. When you see him, please tell your husband we'd like to talk to him and ask him to call us. Thank you for your time and consideration, Mrs. Keighley." And I stood up and handed her my card.

She took it, rather reluctantly, I thought, stared at it dubiously, then looked up at me, smiled and said, "Of course, Mr. Starke. I'll be happy to."

I'm pretty sure that was a lie, but the interview ended, though on a somewhat strained note, and Heather and I left her standing in the doorway staring after us.

"So," Heather said as we walked to the car, "what d'you think, Harry?"

"First," I said, "I think she knows more than she's telling, and it doesn't bode well for her husband. She slipped up badly, and she knows it."

"Yes, I got that," Heather said. "What else?" she said as she climbed into the car.

"Well, one way or another, I think she's involved—"

"You didn't notice, did you?" Heather asked, smiling as she pulled the driver's side door closed.

"Notice?" I frowned. "Notice what?"

The engagement ring on her finger. It's the one missing from the evidence locker."

Now that was a real kick in the guts. "What?" I asked. "How can you be sure?"

"Women tend to notice things like that," she said, grinning. "And it looks very much like it to me. I've seen the evidence photos, the enlargements, so yes, I'm sure. It's one of a kind. I'm surprised you didn't notice it."

"Yeah, me, too," I muttered ruefully. "If it is, and I don't doubt you're right, it could be the break we've been waiting for. I need to call Kate."

And, as Heather pulled out onto the street, I was about to do just that when my phone rang. I looked at the screen. It was a local number, but not one I was familiar with. I was going to decline it, but something told me it might be important, so I answered it.

"Harry Starke," I said.

"Mr. Starke," the male voice said, "my name's James Keighley. I know who you are and what you're doing."

"Hold on a moment, James. I'm going to pull over and put you on speaker so my partner can hear you."

I put the call on hold and, as Heather pulled over, I said, "It's James Keighley. You know him?"

"He's the Keighley's youngest son. He'd be about forty-two, I think."

"Well, he sounds nervous, but he says he wants to talk."

She nodded and pulled into a church parking lot and stopped the car.

I put the phone on speaker and said, "James, are you still there?"

"Yes, sir," the voice said.

"I have you on speaker with my associate Heather. You can speak freely."

"I know what you're doing, Mr. Starke. I also know who killed Liz and Brendan, and I know who put the bomb in your car."

I looked at Heather. Her eyes were wide.

"Who is it, James?" I said, quietly.

"I can't say," he said, "but you'd better back off. I don't want anyone else to die. He'll kill you. I know he will."

"Who'll kill me, James?" I asked.

"I was in love with Liz," he replied. He sounded wistful.

"Did you kill Elizabeth, James?" I asked.

"What? Me? No! I was nineteen. I was a kid. I loved her. And Brendan; he didn't deserve to die like that. He was my friend. They said he was on drugs. He wasn't. They just said that to get rid of him. He knew too much. I can't go on like this. I have to tell someone. He has to be stopped. If he isn't, I'm afraid it's going to be me next—"

I cut him off. "James," I said, gently. "Stop talking and listen. You need to come to my office. Now. D'you hear me?" But all we could hear was the dial tone. He'd hung up.

I called Kate and briefly told her what had happened and asked her to meet us at my office.

34

IT WAS JUST AFTER ONE-THIRTY THAT AFTERNOON WHEN WE arrived back at my offices. Kate, along with Corbin and Samson, arrived a few moments later and we all gathered together in the conference room.

I spent the next twenty minutes describing in detail our interview with Vickie Keighley and that Heather had recognized the ring on her finger as the one that had disappeared from the evidence box. I also gave them the gist of James Keighley's phone call.

The consensus was that the prime suspect for the death of Elizabeth Reynolds, Amy Murphy and Brendan Loftin and the car bomb was Walter Keighley. It was also decided that we still didn't have enough to charge him with any of it. All we had was a slip of the tongue on Vickie's part, a ring that might or might not be the one missing from the evidence locker, and a phone call full of irrational ramblings.

If at the time you were to ask me, as both Jacque and TJ did, I would have said, and did say, that together they made a substantial case. The one thing that was missing, of course, was an official statement made by James Keighley, and to get that, we had to bring him in.

And then, as if he'd been listening in, I received first one email from him and then another.

"See if you can trace then back to an address, Tim," I said.

He nodded and went to work on his laptop.

The first had an attachment, a photograph of a letter—who writes those anymore?—from Elizabeth Reynolds to Walter Keighley, the gist of which was that she never wanted to see him again. That he was "too rough," and that he'd almost "strangled her to death" the last time they'd met.

The second was an email with a rambling repetition of the phone call, but it didn't give a name. The letter was significant. It proved that Elizabeth Reynolds was on intimate terms with Walter Keighley, but it didn't prove he killed her.

The email? It was worthless. But it was now clear that we'd found Elizabeth's secret client. But there was nothing in the letter or the email that indicated Walter saw her on the night that she was murdered.

As the discussion around the table continued, it became clear that we had to talk to James Keighley and find out exactly what he knew, but where was he? He hadn't been there that morning when TJ and Heather had visited the home. Or had he? Maybe he was. Maybe he was hiding.

"I have an address," Tim said. "It's the Keighley's home."

TJ nodded. "How are we going to do this, Harry?" TJ asked.

I looked at Kate.

"We go in force," she said. "You and me to the front door. The rest will stay back out of sight until needed. Hopefully, they won't be. But if the killer is willing to use C-4, he must be pretty desperate, so we should be prepared for the worst."

I nodded and looked around the table. "Everyone happy with that?" I asked, and everyone indicated their agreement. Even Tim.

"Oh, no!" I said. "Not you, Tim. I need you to stay and keep an eye on things with Lucy."

"Aw but—" he began, but I cut him off. "No arguments, Tim. You stay here. Everyone else… Let's go."

IT WAS GETTING on towards three when we arrived at the Keighley home. I traveled with Kate in her unmarked cruiser. My rental had still not arrived.

We left Samson in the cruiser and approached the front door carefully, keeping an eye on the windows, but nothing appeared to be untoward.

I looked at Kate, eyebrows raised in question. She nodded, and I thumbed the doorbell button and we waited, and we waited.

I pushed the button again, and then I hammered on the door with my fist. I was just about to leave Kate and go around the back when the door opened. I say it opened, but it was no more than a crack, and a male voice said, "Who's there?"

"Chattanooga police," Kate said. "We're looking for James Keighley. Is that you?"

The door opened a little further, and the voice said, "Let me see some ID."

Kate held her badge up to the opening and said, "I'm Captain Gazzara. This is Harry Starke. We're here to talk to James Keighley. Is that you? If so, please open the door."

The door opened to reveal a man aged about forty-five, with close-cropped brown hair and a stubbled chin.

"No," he said and took a step back. "I'm Jared Keighley, James' older brother. You'd better come in."

"Where's James?" I asked.

"He's in there," Jared said, pointing to an open door just beyond the foyer.

I followed Kate inside and heard her say, "Oh shit!"

"What?" I said as I stepped up beside her. She was right, but "Oh shit" was an understatement. James Keighley was sitting in a leather wing-back chair, his chin on his chest and the front of his shirt soaked with blood. I didn't have to touch him to know that he was dead. He'd been shot. A single bullet to the heart.

"You'd better call it in," I said.

She nodded, took her phone from her jacket pocket, and made the call.

Me? I went back out into the foyer where Jared was still standing like a wet rag, his shoulders slumped, his hands together over his crotch.

"Who did that, Jared?" I asked, jerking my head in the direction of what I later learned was the parlor.

He shrugged, but didn't answer.

I nodded. He looked at me. I said, "Very well, since you don't want to answer, I'll have to assume it was you. What did you do with the gun?"

"It wasn't me," he whispered. "I found him like that. There was nobody else in the house. I was going to call the police, but you came hammering on the door. I thought it was him coming back."

"You thought it was who coming back?" I asked.

He shrugged. "I don't know. Someone."

It was then that Kate joined us. "We need to take him in for questioning," she said.

"We do," I said, "but I'd like to talk to him here first. If it's who I think it is that shot his brother, we need to know now. He has to be stopped before he kills someone else."

She stared at me for a moment, but then she nodded and turned to Jared and said, "Jared, we'd like to talk to you. You're not under arrest. Do you understand?"

He nodded, and she continued, "I'm going to read you your rights."

Again he nodded, and she began the spiel, "Jared Keighley, you have the right…" and so on. When she was done, she asked him if he understood his rights and if he was willing to talk to us. He said he was, and that he'd done nothing wrong, and that he didn't know who killed his brother.

The house was now a crime scene, so we had to take him outside. I asked him if there was anywhere quiet where we could talk and he nodded at a gazebo in the middle of an ornamental garden, and that's where we went.

But first, while Kate escorted Jared to the gazebo, I went to Corbin and my team, told them what had happened, what we were about to do, that backup was on the way, and that they were to stay put until we knew what we were going to do next. Then I ran to the gazebo where Kate had Jared already seated.

He looked dazed, and I wondered if we were doing the right thing. But we had to know, and quickly.

I sat down on the bench opposite him, leaned forward, and clasped my hands together.

"Who killed your brother, Jared?" Kate asked.

"I don't know," he replied.

"Was it your father?" she asked.

"I said I don't know who killed him," he replied.

"I think you do," I said.

He stared at me, then shook his head and said, "I don't know if he did or not. I wasn't here, and my father wasn't here when I came in. And I don't want to know. I know James hated him for what he thought he did to Elizabeth. They were friends, James and Elizabeth. James was in love with her. But then, Dad…" He paused for a second, then continued, "James thinks he killed her. I think it was through him that Dad met her, but I don't know for sure. I know he was seeing her."

"Do you remember anything about the night Elizabeth died?" Kate asked.

"Not as such," he replied. "I remember watching the TV the following morning. It was on the news. James was out of his mind. He'd heard Dad and Mom arguing the night before, and he told me later he'd gone downstairs, and that Dad had just come home. He heard him yell at Mom that he'd been home all night. James was convinced he'd killed Liz. He's barely spoken to him since. He told me that Liz had told him that Dad was some kind of pervert."

He thought for a moment then said, "The only other thing I remember, and I don't know if it was that night or not… It was around that time, that weekend, that Mom's engagement ring was missing. She played holy hell with him. They had a huge row about it. Mom kept on nagging at him for days. He'd taken it to have it resized and was supposed to have picked it up. She was as mad as a wet hen, raving about the ring and his… indiscretions. They did find it. But it was months later. Where it was, I don't know. That's all I remember. James never got over Liz's death. He swore Dad killed her."

Again, he paused, then said, "He was… different this last week. He knew you'd reopened the investigation. He told me he was going to fix it once and for all, but he never said how. After that, he was distant, you know? Like he had a lot on his mind. And yesterday I heard them yelling at each other, him and Dad. I was upstairs, so I couldn't hear what it was about. It ended up with the front door banging shut. I came downstairs, but James was gone. I asked Dad what was the matter? He mumbled something and then charged out after him. That was the last I saw of either of them until just now."

Kate thought for a moment, then said, "Do you know Amy Murphy, Jared?"

He frowned, shook his head, and said, "No. Who is she?"

"It doesn't matter," Kate replied. "How about Brendan Loftin?"

He looked confused, then said, "He worked for Mom until about six years ago, I think. He was a bit weird. I never had much to do with him. Why, what about him?"

Kate ignored the question. "Where would he have gone, your dad?" she asked.

He shrugged. "Probably to his downtown office. He spends most of his time there."

"Do you have an address?" she asked.

He gave it to her, and she said, "How about a phone number?"

He told her what it was, and she stood up and said, "Thank you, Jared." She paused for a moment, staring down at him, then said, "Look, you're not in any trouble. You're not under arrest, but I have to take you in. Just until we find your father. Do you understand?" He nodded, stood up, and held out his hands.

She smiled at him and said, "There's no need for that, Jared. Come with me and I'll have someone drive you to the police department." Then she looked at me and nodded.

It was five after four.

35

KEIGHLEY'S OFFICE WAS HOUSED IN WHAT ONCE HAD BEEN A stand-alone, one-story retail shop on Broad Street. We arrived in force and parked on the street: Kate and me and Samson in her cruiser, Corbin in his, and TJ and Heather in his black SUV. Jacque had returned to the office.

The doors were, of course, locked. I banged on the door, to no avail. The lights were on, but if he was inside, there was no sign of him, so Kate called the number Jared had given her. She punched in the number and put the phone on speaker.

It rang five or six times before Vickie Keighley answered it.

"Who is this?" she snapped. "The office is closed until Monday. Call back then." And she hung up.

Kate called the number again. This time Vickie picked up almost immediately. "What is it you want?" she asked angrily.

"Is this Mrs. Keighley? If it is, please don't hang up. Is your husband there?"

"No, he is not," she snapped. "Now—"

"We need to talk to you about your son, James," Kate said. "Please open the door."

There was a moment of silence during which I thought I could hear her talking to someone.

"What about James," she said, eventually.

"We can't do this over the phone, Mrs. Keighley," Kate said. "You need to let us in."

"Umm… Er… I… No. I—" The phone went dead.

There was another long silence while we were discussing what to do next when we heard a scream inside.

Kate looked at me. I nodded, stood back and… what I didn't see was the pair of eyes staring out of the glass panel at the top of the door, but Kate did.

I ran at the door, shoulder first.

"*Harry! Stop!*" Kate yelled.

But it was too late. Just as my shoulder was about to hit the door, it opened. I stumbled inside and it closed again. I recovered quickly, but found myself facing a tall, well-built, gray-haired man with a gun in his hand.

"Harry Starke, I presume," he said, smiling.

"Mr. Keighley. Nice to meet you, sir. Why don't you put the gun away so we can talk things over calmly?"

The weapon was a nickel-plated, compact SIG Sauer 1911, a .45 and, if it was anything like the pair Bob Ryan used to carry, it had a hair trigger.

"As if," he said. "Don't try anything stupid. If you do…" He glanced down at the gun and left the rest of the warning unsaid.

"Sit down," he said, motioning toward a chair with the weapon.

It was then I noticed Mrs. Keighley. She'd been standing at the back of the room. In my confusion, as I rushed inside, I hadn't noticed her.

He stepped quickly forward, put the gun to my head, relieved me of my weapon, and then stepped quickly away.

"Grab the duct tape from the bottom drawer of my desk and tape his wrists together behind his back," he snapped.

"Wh...at?" she quavered.

"You heard me," he snapped. "Do it."

It was then that the phone rang. He snatched it up, held it to his ear, and snapped, "Don't even think about busting in here? Do it and Starke's a dead man." And he slammed the receiver back in its cradle.

"I said tie his hands," he yelled at her.

"I can't," she sobbed. "I can't get them together properly."

"Oh, for God's sake, woman. Do them in front then and tape 'em up tight," he snarled. "And you. Put your hands together, asshole.

I grinned up at him, but didn't move.

He stepped up beside me and put the muzzle of the gun to my ear and said, Put your frickin' hands together or I'll shoot you in the frickin' head."

"Tsk, tsk," I said as I did as he ordered. "That temper's going to get you into trouble one of these days." I grinned up at him as his wife taped my wrists together in front of me.

He watched her finish, then stepped away and said, "You're one nosey son of a bitch, Starke. Do you know that? Why couldn't you have just let things be?"

"It's not in my nature," I said. "By the way, does your wife know you killed your son James?"

"*Noooo*," she screamed and ran at him and began beating on his chest with her fists. He struck her a single blow to the right side of her face that sent her staggering across the room. She slammed against the wall, turned around, and slid to the ground.

"That was a manly thing to do, Walter," I said. "I think you may have broken her jaw."

"Screw you, Starke," he said, and went and sat down behind his desk, the gun still in his right hand.

"You can't for one minute think you're going to get away with this," I said. "The police are already outside."

"Shut the hell up," he snapped.

"You killed them all, didn't you?" I asked. "Elizabeth Reynolds. She was the first. Then what happed?"

"You!" he snarled. "You're what happened. None of this would have happened if it hadn't been for you. Now my son is dead, and that's on you, Starke."

"Oh, no!" I said and laughed at him. "You pulled the trigger. How does it feel, Walter, to know that you killed your own son?"

"He wouldn't stop talking," Keighley said angrily. "He wouldn't… stop. He said he was going to tell you about what happened that night."

"What a shame," I said. "You killed the boy for nothing."

"What?" he glared at me across the desk.

I shook my head, smiling at him, and said, "You killed him for nothing. I already knew what happened that night. We went to your home to arrest you," I lied. "We knew about your wife's ring. It was found at the scene of Elizabeth's murder. Who was it that returned it to you? Whacker? Finkle? My boss, Tom Miller? Unfortunately for you, whoever it was left the photographs. Your wife was wearing it when we interviewed her."

I glanced at her. She was sobbing loudly, her hands to her face, the ring front and center.

"See," I said.

"You stupid bitch," he yelled. "I knew I should never have given it back to you. Oh shit! Oh shit, shit, shit!"

"So, all those bodies," I said, reasonably. "Elizabeth, Amy, Brendan, James, and you almost got me, too, when you put that C-4 in my car."

"I didn't do that," he snapped. "I hired someone to do that. An explosives expert." He sounded… resigned, tired.

I grinned at him. "Life gets tedious, doesn't it, Walter? Come on. Give it up, man. You can't win this one."

He didn't answer. He just sat there, staring at the 1911.

I knew what he was thinking. I also knew I had to keep him talking.

"Why did you kill Elizabeth, Walter?"

He looked up at me. He was holding the gun in his right hand and was fingering the barrel with the other. I didn't like it, not one bit.

"I didn't mean to," he replied, absently. "It was an accident. I… I…"

"He can't, is what he's trying to say," his wife yelled. "He's frickin' impotent. The only way he can do it is if he chokes them."

"Shut up, you stupid bitch," he yelled and grabbed the desk phone and threw it across the room at her. Fortunately, it missed her.

"It was an accident," he said.

"And Amy Murphy?" I asked. "Did you pump her full of xylazine by accident, too?"

"Shut the hell up, Starke." The gun twitched in his hand.

"Hey," I said. "Is that sirens I hear? They're coming for you, Walter. Oh boy. You're in trouble, my friend."

"I'm not your frickin' friend, asshole," he snapped.

"Give up, Walter," I said, "before someone else gets killed. At least let your wife go."

He glanced at her but said nothing.

"So, who was it you hired to bomb my car?" I asked. "I loved that car."

"Pity you weren't in it," he said, then took a deep breath, closed his eyes and slowly raised the gun toward his head.

It was what I'd been waiting for. I immediately raised my arms high above my head, tensed my gut, then brought my arms down as hard as I could, using my stomach to force my wrists apart. The tape tore. My hands were free. I leapt to my feet, hurled myself across his desk, grabbed his gun hand in both of mine and forced it back away from his head, but not before he pulled the trigger.

The gun, now pointed back and away, fired one, twice, three times, before I could wrest it away from him. All the bullets went through the ceiling and into the roof.

And, just as I did, the door burst open and Corbin and Samson came rushing in, followed by Kate. But by then, it was too late. I had him on the floor with his arm so far up his back he could have grabbed his own collar.

He screamed with pain as I hauled him to his feet.

It was, as my old grandmother would have said, all over but the shouting; in this case, the interview.

36

Walter Keighley and his wife were taken to the police department on Amnicola, where they were installed in separate interview rooms and questioned.

Me? I wasn't allowed to attend either of the interviews, but I was allowed into the observation room where the chief, Corbin, and I watched Kate interview Walter.

He lawyered up, of course, but that didn't stop him from talking. At first, he admitted nothing. Then he reluctantly admitted causing the death of Elizabeth Reynolds, though he claimed it was an accident, and he was totally indifferent about it.

He never admitted to the deaths of Amy Murphy or Brendan Loftin, and we were unable to prove otherwise. Nor did he admit to bombing my car, even though he'd admitted it to me, and in front of his wife. She refused to talk at all, and without a name, we couldn't get him for that either.

As to the death of his son, James, he claimed that was an accident, too. And he did seem genuinely remorseful, at least about the death of his son.

Why did he go to such great lengths to get the ring? Well, as it turned out, it wasn't because he thought the ring might one day incriminate him, as it actually did. It was because he loved his wife. Theirs was a tumultuous relationship. A genuine love-hate affair. He was, of course, examined by a forensic psychiatrist who deemed him a narcissistic psychopath with a psychosomatic sexual disorder. Charming, right?

And then there was Henry Finkle. Walter had given him up, along with Whacker and my old boss, Tom Miller. All three had been on the take to a lesser or greater degree. It had been Gordon Whacker who'd taken the ring from the evidence locker. His reward? Five thousand in cash. Tom's only involvement was his protection of not only Elizabeth Reynolds but also several of the other escorts; all in return for sexual favors. He'd been having a high old time all the way up to his retirement. But back to Henry.

I wasn't there, but I got the story from Kate, who was. Johnston called Finkle into his office and laid the facts before him, then he gave him a choice: either take early retirement or be fired. He took retirement. Which was a good thing. The scandal of him being fired would have been a black moment for the PD, and the chief couldn't have that.

It was much the same for Miller. He was a minor player. But Whacker. Well, he'd stolen a valuable item from the evidence room. He copped a plea and was fined a thousand dollars and was given a six-month suspended sentence. It was no big deal. In other words, it was neatly covered up without a scandal. Nice, but one has to wonder how it would have gone if it had been a uniformed officer instead of a retired senior assistant chief.

Walter? He was charged with the second-degree murder of Elizabeth Reynolds and the negligent homicide of his son, James, for which he received life imprisonment for the first and five years for the second.

His wife Vickie was never charged with anything, and, to my knowledge, she's never spoken about it since. Neither has her son Jared.

David Archer was set free just in time for Christmas, almost six weeks after Walter's arrest. I was there for his release. MaryAnn was there to pick him up. The press was also there in force, but David refused to speak to them, though he did speak to me.

David was… angry. He refused to shake my hand.

"Twenty-one years, Starke," he said bitterly. "That's what you stole from me. I hope you can live with yourself knowing what you did."

"I know," I said, "and I'm truly sorry. I know that's not enough. But, for what it's worth, if there's anything you need; if there's anything I can do for you, you only have to call."

He simply nodded and turned away, and I didn't blame him. I felt like shit. No kidding. It was a good day, but it was also one of the worst, at least for me.

I drove back to Chattanooga that day in a kind of fugue. His words had hit me hard, and I couldn't help but wonder how many more innocent men and women were in prison for something they didn't do.

It was a Wednesday. I should have been celebrating. Bob Ryan had been back for more than a month, which was… great, but it wasn't the same. He'd changed. I'd changed. We'd all changed. The past was… the past, and there was no reliving it. I was… I don't know what I was. But I was changed, that I knew for a fact. The David Archer case was a devastating blow, and I didn't know if I'd ever recover from it.

Amanda was, as she always was, there for me. We talked into the night frequently, and the only solution we could come up with was that I needed a break, and with Bob back, I felt I could take a little time off. And I did. We went back to Calypso Key, the island in the Caribbean where we were married, and spent two idyllic weeks of sun, sand, sea and sailing.

Me? As I sat on the sand the final day of our vacation, I

couldn't help but think of Scarlett O'Hara's final words in *Gone With The Wind*:

Tomorrow is another day.

Thank you for reading ***Unfinished Business,*** the twenty-fourth book in the Harry Starke Novels. I hope you enjoyed it, if you did please help others find Blair Howards Books by leaving a few words about it in the form of a review.

HARRY STARKE WILL BE BACK WITH HIS NEXT CASE SOON!

DON'T MISS THIS

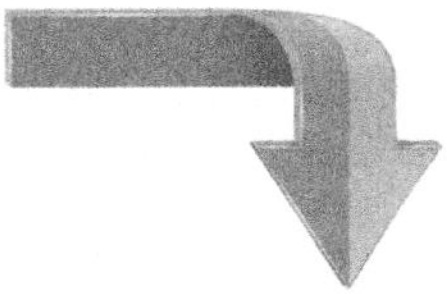

From Blair Howard

The Harry Starke Genesis Series

The Harry Starke Series

The Lt. Kate Gazzara Murder Files

Randall & Carver Mysteries

The Peacemaker Series

The Civil War Series

From Blair C. Howard

The Sovereign Star Series

ABOUT THE AUTHOR

Blair Howard is a retired journalist turned novelist. He's the author of more than 50 novels including the international best-selling Harry Starke series of crime stories, the Lt. Kate Gazzara series, and the Harry Starke Genesis series. He's also the author of the Peacemaker series of international spy thrillers and five Civil War/Western novels.

If you enjoy reading Science Fiction thrillers, Mr. Howard has made his debut into the genre with, The Sovereign Stars Series under the name, Blair C. Howard.

Visit www.blairhowardbooks.com.

You can also find Blair Howard on Social Media

Print ISBN: 979-8-9908529-2-1
Cleveland, TN

Printed in Great Britain
by Amazon

48556194R00139